The Web of Easter Island

By Donald Wandrei

- Ecstasy
- Dark Odyssey
- The Eye and the Finger
- The Web of Easter Island

The Web
of
Easter Island

BY

DONALD WANDREI

ARKHAM HOUSE   SAUK CITY, WISCONSIN

1948

Contents

To H. P. Lovecraft

The Web of Easter Island

I

MYSTERY AT ISLING

THE Vadia is an old, stone road that rambles past the village of Isling. It skirts Isling toward the west until it reaches the graveyard. There it comes to an abrupt end, but a dirt lane follows the hawthorn hedge around the graveyard to a point opposite, where the Vadia continues.

Legend has it that the Vadia was used by legionaries in the days of Roman occupation, and that it had been built long even before the imperial army came. Archaeologists place no credit in the legend; according to them, the Picts and Gaels who roamed the wild hills and lowlands were incapable of such an engineering feat. But many a legend stems from origins unknown to archaeology, and folklore has often proved itself based on forgotten facts.

Isling is full of legends, mostly centering around the Vadia. According to one tradition, its very name is a corruption of the Latin, Via Dei. Those who believe the tradition point to the graveyard which dates back no man knows how far. Others assert that the name derives from Via Diaboli, and support their conviction by the break in the road at the graveyard. Still others say the Vadia is just a name with no special significance.

Until that day when the first lock opened on the great crypt of time, the legends seemed only as veils of enchantment attached to things olden and vanished. To be sure,

Roman coins had occasionally been found, together with bits of pottery; and once, in the digging of a new grave, certain objects had been cast up which caused the vicar to place his stamp against the whole graveyard and order new ground dedicated. That happened during the reign of Elizabeth. A hundred years later when the Great Plague swept across the land, and the dead outnumbered the survivors at Isling, a mass grave was hastily prepared in the old burial ground, but for some obscure reason no interments followed, and the authorities re-filled the empty hole.

Ever since, the ground had remained an unused relic of the past. Its most recent headstones, of the sixteenth century, though worn and fallen away, yet seemed strangely new compared with older stones weathered beyond all recognition of markings, and still more antique vaults said to lie deep under the surface, covered now with the earth changes of dozens of centuries before recorded time.

Rumor said that blasphemous rites had flourished during the years of Roman occupation, with orgies to powers and beings greater than mortal, that in other ages Druid rituals had fulfilled the ecstasies and terrors of the forest. But the only known documentary reference dates from the year 1665, in the register of John Clelonde: "This day, nineteen more poor wretches buried, nor are the women and children spared. The wrath of God continues unabated. I did command them all not yet stricken to give their souls to the keeping of our Lord, and to pray that his vengeance be lifted. The shops all be closed. Nor does any man venture abroad, lest he be smitten of this pestilence. We are hard pressed to bury the dead. The ground new broke is already filled, and we durst not use the Devil's Graveyard, by reason of the accursed image found there this day week, though the pit lies open."

This mention of an image may have contributed to the growth of the legends, in the way that oral tradition has preserved folklore from periods when images fixed on tablets of the mind formed the only records of man.

These legends began to assume a new significance when, in the late afternoon of a muggy July day, eleven-year-old Willy Grant returned to his cottage and proudly showed a little object he had found.

"What is it?" asked his mother, blinking her weary eyes as she turned from cutting a few selected roses in her flower garden.

"I dunno. Me an' Bill an' Jack found it, but I got it first, so it's mine."

"Where did you find it?"

The boy hesitated a minute. "Oh, we all went into the old graveyard when Bill dared us an' I saw it stickin' in the ground so I pulled it out an' brought it along."

"Give it to me," she commanded in that final tone of voice with which there is no arguing. Reluctantly, Willy handed it over. She immediately hurled it toward the roadway. "Tomorrow," she continued in the same tone, "you take it back where it came from and throw it over the hedge. Then, if you ever go near that graveyard again, you'll get the strapping of your life. Now into the house with you."

Willy whined and pleaded, but his mother would not listen. Superstitious Mrs. Grant repeated that if he ever went near the graveyard again or had anything more to do with the object, he would be whipped blue.

Near nightfall, John Grant came home from the day's toil of delivering mail. While he took off his heavy walking shoes, Mrs. Grant scurried around preparing the evening meal. She said nothing to her husband about Willy's discovery. Perhaps she had forgotten about it already, nor did she notice that the boy had slipped away for a minute and returned to his room furtively carrying something.

After the meal, the rest of the evening passed with the small talk that had concluded their every monotonous day for a dozen years. At nine-thirty sharp, Willy was sent to bed, and at ten John and Madge Grant followed, in the unvarying routine of their existence. The night hung still, but hot and damp. John Grant, a tiredness in his legs, quickly dropped off to sleep. His wife lay restless, and for a long time remained awake, but towards midnight she too finally sank into a troubled slumber.

For the first time in many months, she dreamed a dream; and her dream had an extraordinary and terrifying nature such as she had never before experienced. She thought she went walking past a graveyard where hundreds of old, white tombstones rose eerie everywhere. She wanted to run away, but the mesmeric power of dreamland held her. While she watched, a curious small gray thing with the face of her son scuttled across the burial ground and pulled a carven image from the earth. As it did so, the white tombstones suddenly turned into carven images and soared skyward until an army of colossal, implacable monsters stood before her. And beneath their feet, the tombs opened up and discovered vast corridors leading into the bowels of earth, and from their immeasurable depths rose the stench of ancient corruption. The thing with the face of Willy scampered away bearing its prize. She tried to cry out and warn it to drop its burden, but no sound came from her throat. The little beast scurried toward the safety of a blob of devouring darkness. Now the titans moved with great strides, to block that escape, until they formed a circle around the gray creature. Slowly, slowly, the giant limbs closed inexorably on the captive, the ring became smaller, impassive Gargoyle faces stared on the animal that whimpered wildly around trying to escape. She saw it forced toward the rim of a bottomless corridor, nearer, nearer—

From the realms of sleep, John Grant and Madge Grant awoke at the same instant, their ears filled with a shriek of terror. John Grant leaped from his bed and raced to Willy's room while old Madge lighted a lamp with trembling hands and followed. She heard her husband call, "What is it, son?" But she heard no answer. She brought him the lamp, and together they looked in.

John Grant gave a hoarse gasp, but his wife made no sound as she slumped to the floor. The lamp crashed, and tongues of flame began to dance. Faced with a choice of the living from the dead, he carried his wife to safety. The grotesque form on the bed, of changing outline and phosphorescent shine, green and pitted as if some enormous worm had gnawed, bore little resemblance to the Willy who had been theirs; and the black, liquid eyes that stared blindly at them were never those of their son. John

Grant gave silent prayer as the cottage burned to the ground.

Old Madge was Mad Madge when she became conscious. She mumbled of a "green little big stone that ate Willy", and the neighbors shook their heads pityingly. She took to wandering along the Vadia, and prowling around the graveyard, with her hair matted and her eyes glary. If asked what she sought, she would answer that she was hunting for the green stone that ate Willy. Had she not been insane, her reply might have drawn persistent questions from the curious; but they considered her words the raving of a demented woman. John Grant remained taciturn. He chose to let the villagers think that his son had died in an unfortunate but accidental fire.

The days slipped by, one torpid afternoon following another as July drew to a close. A fortnight after the tragedy some of the neighbors saw Mad Madge running down the Vadia in the early twilight. She carried an object wrapped with her shawl, and gasped as if she had run far. She turned from the roadway and stumbled toward the vacant cottage which she and her husband were temporarily occupying.

As she entered the house, she found her husband already waiting. He looked at her with surprise and pity, noticing her disheveled appearance and the bundle she hugged tightly.

"What is it, Madge? What is it you have there?" he asked kindly.

She sucked the air and raved incoherently that she had found Willy. A weird light of madness and joy glittered in her eyes, she clutched the shawl closer to her breast, she crooned meaningless phrases over it. John tried to see what it was that she carried, but she backed away snarling and hugged the object still more tightly. The shawl became loosened momentarily when she sat in a chair, but all he could see of what she held was that it seemed gray, or possibly greenish. She rocked back and forth, back and forth incessantly, talking and muttering to herself. John heard a phrase that got on his nerves, "The little green stone that ate Willy," repeated over and over, together with mumbled pleas that something would "Please give back Willy, he didn't mean any harm by it."

Throughout the evening, heat lightning flickered in the sky, the air hung sultry and heavy. Clouds were piling up from the west, and it seemed as if a dry spell of weeks at last would be broken. Just after nightfall, the first big drops fell. There followed a minute's hush, then the wind arose, and gusts of rain whipped against the windows.

At bedtime, Mad Madge let herself be led away, carrying the object still wrapped in the shawl. John made another half-hearted attempt to discover its nature and take it from her, but decided rather to humor her, when she drew her lips back like an animal at his slightest gesture toward the shawl.

She held the bundle even in bed, like a child with its doll. John heard her talking for a long time, till her voice finally died out. He lay awake a while after, thinking back on the mysterious death of Willy, and what to do with Madge. He wondered if it might not be that both of them were mad, and the whole occurrence merely a dream of delirium. What power could have caused so malignant and monstrous a change in Willy? Perhaps it resulted from some dreadful disease that gave no warning symptoms until it had progressed beyond hope of cure. He would never know, now; only that it must have been for the best that death came quickly. The ways of the Lord proved inscrutable.

The wind prowled around the house and whooped through the trees. Invisible fingers moved the shutters. Squalls of rain from time to time swirled against the windows. To the accompaniment of these elemental sounds, John was dozing off when he heard his wife begin to mumble again. He looked at her during a brief lightning flare. Though her eyes remained closed, her lips moved.

"N'ga n'ga rhthl'g clr'tl—"

What fantastic gibberish was this that came from Madge? It seemed meaningless. He could not recognize a single familiar word in that harsh jargon of consonants and breathings, nor did the low voice sound like that of his wife as it went on in a kind of rhythmic chant, "—ust s g'lgggar septhulchu nyrcg—"

During the night, giant bolts of lightning fissured the sky. Disturbed by the violence of the storm, a Mrs. Sayres whose home lay nearest to the temporary quarters of the Grants awakened just in time to see a dazzling flare envelope their house with a crash as of bursting worlds. She thought she saw a vast green smudge sprawl off the roof. During the intensity of blackness that followed, she stood with nose flattened against her window till the lightning crackled anew. The sky's reflected glare showed the house still standing, and no trace of that strange, great shadow, though she convinced herself that the previous

bolt had struck the house by the Vadia. A furious down-
pour now completely obscured her view. Satisfied no harm
had befallen the Grants, since she had not detected a sign
of fire or visible damage, and deterred by the wild night,
she returned to bed.

John Grant did not appear at work the following day.
Nor did Mad Madge come forth. In any small town or
village the world over, the neighbors' affairs are a vital
part of everyone's existence; and when no sign of life
became evident in the Grants' home by mid morning,
idle curiosity developed into more immediate concern.

Several gossips remembered having seen mad Madge
run down the Vadia clutching some object tightly.

"And you know," said garrulous Mrs. Dakin, "Jack said
he and Willy Grant and the Stacy boy went into the graveyard, let me see now, it must have been a fortnight ago,
or maybe three weeks. Well, and they found something,
that is, Willy did, and took it home with him, and Jack
says it wasn't like anything he ever saw before, a funny
little stone man only it wasn't a man at all. I always did
say no good came out of the old graveyard, and now here
it's proved before our eyes, the Lord's got his curse against
it. Why you know their cottage burned to the ground that
very night and poor Willy with it, and John had a great
to-do to get Madge out in time, and now there's no telling
what's happened to the both of them, poor souls. Something dreadful, you may be sure."

"Maybe they're dead," added Mrs. Sayres helpfully.
"When I saw that big bolt strike, I says to myself, says I,
'It's a good thing it wasn't you that it hit,' meaning me,

of course. Like as not both got killed or hurt bad, and they're up there now waiting for somebody to come after them.

"Of course," she tacked on apologetically, "I couldn't go out in that terrible storm, there's no saying what might have happened to me, it was that bad."

"It's just possible," put in one of the more intelligent townsmen, "that Mad Madge got terrified of the storm and ran off, with John out searching for her. You never know about those things. Seems to me we ought to wait a while. I don't like to put my nose in other folk's troubles."

"Well, I don't like the looks of it," went on Mrs. Dakin, "and if I had my way I'd have been gone from Isling all these years just to get away from that Devil's Graveyard. Why, the storm woke me up last night and made such a racket you never heard in all your born days, and I thought somebody was shouting outside but I couldn't understand a word of it. I never did like these foreigners, anyway, English is good enough for me and it's good enough for anybody, I think."

It was finally agreed that an investigation ought to be made. Three men elected to find out what had happened, or whether the Grants needed aid.

They walked up to the house and pounded on the door, but only the echo of their knocking answered them. They shouted to John and Madge, inquiring if they wanted assistance, but no voice came back to them. In the pause that followed they held a short consultation and agreed that duty now required them to enter.

The door had not been locked. They opened it, to be met by a heavy, nauseating stench that forced them to retreat until the foul air had partly cleared away. When they finally re-entered, the sickening odor compelled them to breathe through handkerchiefs.

A hurried search of the ground floor disclosed nothing amiss. They halted again at the entrance for breaths of fresh air, then climbed to the bedroom. Its door was closed. They pushed it, but though unlocked, it did not yield. A weight lay against it from the inside. With growing suspicions of what they might find, they put their shoulders against it and heaved it open far enough to enter. They could hear the weight dragging as they shoved it back.

In the room they found one body half-fallen from bed, and another that seemed to have been clawing at the door which provided no escape. Madge's shawl lay empty on the floor; whatever she had wrapped in it had vanished.

Mad Madge and John Grant were dead, if indeed those forms had been theirs. For in that mass of greenish corruption, gouged and pitted, remained little of human resemblance. Before their horrified eyes, the bodies gave the illusion that they underwent a final transformation, as though shimmering in heat-waves, melting and changing from flesh to a less stable state, from man to beast to stone, a strange and awesome impression that sent the three searchers running downstairs.

An inquest was held; the verdict returned, "Death by lightning." Unanswerable questions went unasked. How could lightning have caused so profound a change? Why had not the bodies charred or burned? What was it that Mad Madge held as she ran down the Vadia? Whose voice had rumbled guttural syllables while the storm raged? And if death had not resulted from lightning, what unimaginable agency wrought that metamorphosis of flesh? Nothing known to man could have brought about so rapid and total an alteration in the very organic structure of the two corpses. Against his will to believe, the village doctor denied that Madge and John might have fallen victims to disease. In his practice, in his experience, and in his medical studies, he had never encountered a case that bore the slightest relation to the baffling condition of the bodies.

The absence of strangers in Isling did not preclude, but argued against, a theory of homicidal attack. The absence of any known motive or any possible motive served only to make the riddle more inexplicable. For the analysis indicated many violences: exposure to heat of the order of suns, and to cold of the intensity of absolute zero; subjection to pressures as high as the bottom of oceans, and to vacuum as complete as the far spaces between stars.

Death by lightning seemed reasonable for the record, though it offered no explanation to those four who had viewed the bodies. Isling accepted this substitution of the familiar for the incredible. But the legends of the past lived again; and the new riddle provided a basis for legends to haunt the future.

Through the medium of a sensation-loving daily newspaper, an account of the mystery at Isling reached the public. Thus the incident came to the attention of Carter E. Graham, curator of the Ludbury Museum of Archaeology and Anthropology.

II

THE DEVIL'S GRAVEYARD

GRAHAM'S coffee cooled on the table, and his toast was already cold, but he had forgotten them. Could the time be near? The time for which his researches, and a theory, had prepared him? He read again the half-column story about the mystery at Isling, a narrative that held extraordinary interest for him.

Graham was in his early forties. Though spare rather than tall, his slender build emphasized his stature. Both in action and in repose his manner suggested the careful thought with which he had prepared his way.

Now, having read the newspaper account for a second time, he sat for several minutes with a far-away look in his eyes, reflecting on memories newly aroused. The images that fleeted through his mind in those few minutes hardly seemed relevant to what he had just read. He thought of explorations he had made in Egypt, in Tibet, at Stonehenge, among the Mayan remains, and on Easter Island. Perhaps he would one day publish the results of his work, but he had never yet condensed those notes. After his early researches and the ending of the inheritance that had made them possible, he settled down to his present occupation, and to occasional study of Roman relics in England; but now a newspaper story brought a resurgence of his past absorption in a cosmic riddle connected with certain ancient remains found among different parts of the world.

Reference to a small image, said to have been discovered by several boys and to have disappeared since, was the sole point in the Isling affair to which his thoughts kept returning again and again; for if that image proved what he believed it to be, he might yet take a long step further on his quest of other years.

"Can it be possible?" he asked himself. "At Isling—less than a hundred miles away. And I have travelled to the ends of earth! Of course, the reporter may have erred—you never can separate truth from imagination in news stories. Well, there's only one way to find out."

He crossed quickly to the telephone and called the train station. His connection was made in a few seconds.

"Hello! At what time does the next train leave for Isling, Wiltshire?" He glanced at his wrist watch. "At 11:25? And it arrives—at 1:40? Thank you."

It was now a quarter before nine. He used the telephone again, to inform the Museum of his absence, then set swiftly to work, packing a bag with the necessities for a short trip, possibly even an overnight stay.

Before departing, he examined a map of England. His memory had not failed him—Isling lay in the Stonehenge country.

The journey seemed tedious to his eager mind; he passed the hours reflecting on those of his past excavations which might be connected with the incident at Isling. Promptly at one-forty, the train reached Westmor, the station for Isling which lay several miles north. After inquiring when return trains could be caught, he obtained a hack for the rest of his journey. He made his plans before he arrived at Isling. They largely concerned going about his business quietly and avoiding curiosity-seekers on this preliminary survey, unless he found it desirable to make excavations.

It was more than half after two when he alighted at his destination, a hamlet of only a few hundred inhabitants. He could tell instantly that his arrival would be old news within the hour: Isling looked like that kind of a town. But it made no special difference to him, except that his beloved privacy would not exist.

An extra one-pound note persuaded the hack-driver to wait until eight o'clock for his return. He expected to finish his task well before then, but if he did not, he could still dismiss the hack and obtain lodging for the night in Isling.

He saw no need to ask for directions in so small a village. Carrying the bag he had brought with him, Graham walked to the Vadia, which the newspaper account had told him skirted Isling on its west side, and proceeded northward along its course. He noted, in passing, the blackened foundation of a house that had recently burned.

The Devil's Graveyard lay perhaps three-quarters of a mile from the point where he first stepped on the old stone roadbed. He viewed with interest how the Vadia came to an abrupt end a few yards from the cemetery gate. Either the burial ground was actually of greater antiquity than the road, or part of the road had been torn up to make room for it. The alternatives seemed equally implausible.

The relationship of road to cemetery might be worth

future investigation, but for the present he let it pass. There remained approximately four hours of daylight in which to make his survey, for his watch indicated almost three when he entered the cemetery. The afternoon, though very hot and humid, disclosed but a faint haze over distant hills. He welcomed the light, and the hum of an occasional bee.

Entering the cemetery, he had a sudden queer feeling that he had cut himself off from the world. This mood he ascribed to the presence of a high hawthorn hedge that completely enclosed the cemetery except for the entrance gate.

Setting his bag down, he opened it and removed a small collapsible spade, a short-handled pick, and a geologist's hammer. These implements he placed alongside the bag, before examining the field.

The site was unevenly circular and about two hundred yards in diameter, he estimated. It covered the top of a low hill which sloped away gently in all directions. Years had obviously passed since anyone had taken care of the grave-yard; weeds and brambles overran it, discolored head-stones tilted sidewise or had fallen entirely, and several faint indentations marked where wooden caskets had finally been reclaimed by earth. Graham walked completely around the burial ground, analyzing its features and glancing at inscriptions as he walked along. Many of the words were illegible, but among those he could decipher, none dated after the time of Elizabeth.

Satisfied with his tour of inspection which ended where he had begun, he lifted up his spade and pick with a directness of purpose as if he had located what he wanted, and made his way to the slightly higher central ground. He again looked carefully around him after he had reached his chosen site. A disappointed frown came into his face.

"This is odd," he thought; "something must be wrong. Unless I've been on a wild-goose chase all my life, I ought to have located an altar or possibly a monument here. But there's nothing, absolutely nothing."

He stood perplexed, for he could find no indications that a monument of any kind had ever occupied the spot. But as he continued to survey the vicinity, his searching eyes caught signs indicating that the weeds and even soil had been recently disturbed. Trampled vegetation over an area scarcely two feet in breadth, and freshly turned earth at the center, were all he saw, but they sufficed.

He donned gloves, scraped away the weeds, and with his spade began patiently removing dirt, a little at a time. He had dug only a few inches down when he struck something that gave out a dull, semi-metallic sound. He dropped the spade and used his hands for methodically scooping away the soil. A greenish gray surface came into view. His hands moved more carefully. Sweat ran down his cheeks. Another minute's patient work was enough.

Nothing ever received more gentle handling than the object which he lifted from the shallow hole.

For the period while Graham examined his find, a mixture of surprise, intense concentration, and loathing alternately or together assumed expression on his features. A shadow seemed to obscure the sun, day darkened around him and time opened its ancient portals. He held in his hands an image about four inches high, of enormous weight, carved from some substance unknown to him,

apparently neither of metal nor stone, but of a borderland
between the two. Tiny pits covered its surface, pits that
formed part of its essential design. Greasy green in color,
it exuded an essence of corruption and decay. But its
most abnormal aspect lay in the illusion it gave: it tingled
his hands with a quality of alien force, almost of life, as
though it could change from stone to metal, from metal
to some more primeval, enigmatic stuff. His hands grasped
the image firmly; his eyes saw its outline waver in the
suggestion of strange mutations; and each beginning or
end when it shifted backward through cosmic and forgotten eons of time before ever the races of man peopled
earth, old even when a molten world flamed out of nebu-
lary fires, he thought that it mushroomed above him and
absorbed him as it expanded skyward like a titan of the
stars.

Carter Graham had seen many curious or terrifying
things during the course of his travels; but he had never
known fear until the moment he held in his hands this
image out of oblivion, an image that suggested in no
single way and yet in all ways age beyond comprehension.
His head aswirl from emotional reaction to the little
horror, he felt an impulse to bury it again, and for ever.

With a slow, heavy effort, he succeeded in throwing off
the depression that had come over him. He deliberately
laid the image aside and turned his attention once more
to the excavation he had started. His past experience told
him to go deeper, for the great finds of archaeology seldom
came from the surface. Instinct warned him to go no
farther. He lifted his spade and resumed digging.

Fifteen minutes, a half-hour, an hour passed in slow

toil and the salt of sweat. He consumed a couple of tablets, and a few swallows of warm water, from the canteen in his bag. Six o'clock came, and six-thirty; not more than a half-hour remained if he intended to find his hack at Isling and catch a return train from Westmor. He had given up hope of making further discoveries, when a blow of his pick brought answer in the same dull, semi-metallic sound given off by the image.

Graham had not expected to encounter a second image; surprise showed plainly on his face. As rapidly as possible, but working with care, he shovelled the soil out. He could not have dug much longer, for the sake of any discovery; fatigue had come, and a sharp hunger. The sun was fast westering, and he labored in a half-gloom.

Beneath him there gradually appeared a flat surface of the same green substance which composed the image; he had not uncovered a second statuette after all. His watch indicated a quarter before seven. He removed several more scoops of dirt, then dropped on his knees to examine the patch which lay exposed.

An expression of bewilderment came into his face. He seemed merely to have added another archaeological mystery to those that the world already knew. Characters unlike any picture, sign, or alphabet writing with which he was familiar cut deeply into the slab on two opposite sides. A group of geometric symbols, in non-Euclidean form, divided the halves of the inscription.

The more he studied his find, the less it meant to him. He felt as philologists must have felt in the presence of hieroglyphs before discovery of the Rosetta stone. He regretted that he had not brought a camera with him. He took a last glance, and ran his fingers lightly over the symbols.

The very earth began to move. The slab tilted and yet without changing its plane; it became an angle, an arc, an oval, a linear point, it collapsed and dissolved in a manner that defied all rules of geometry. Graham caught one appalling glimpse of blackness below him, of a corridor that plunged through measureless depths, he heard the stir of a wind, and to his nostrils came the air of a tomb before Egypt. That same instant, as he clutched at the inscriptions of the slab, the re-transformation occurred. The geometrical enigma reversed itself. He found himself kneeling on a slab of solid. . . . Of solid. . . . Of solid what?

Graham climbed out of the hole and rested for a minute to recover his poise. He observed wryly that his hands could tremble. He stood upright with an effort and began replacing as much soil as he could. Twilight and air, hard work and the feel of the spade handle helped restore his perspective. He developed a positive satisfaction in cascading dirt upon the slab of green.

He kept the small figurine, and when he put his tools away, he wrapped the statuette in a piece of cloth.

He had not attempted to conceal the signs of his digging. He saw no reason to restore completely the disturbed soil. The aspect of the cemetery suggested the passing of weeks and months between visitors. An atmosphere of timelessness, an area of separation from mortal affairs, lay within the confines of the hawthorn hedge.

He experienced anew a deep fatigue, for his labors had been considerable. He felt also the stir of a strong excitement. He believed he stood at the threshold of major discovery. One thing was certain: he would require assistance to continue his explorations in the Devil's Graveyard, but such assistance would be difficult to obtain at Isling. It would serve his purposes best to deposit the weird figurine at the Museum, perhaps to study it in microscopic detail for a day or two. He wanted to compare it with reproductions in various works of authority on the primitive art of Africa, Central America, and Oceania.

The haze at the horizon had grown thicker with twilight, but no change in the oppressive heat accompanied the setting sun. His last glance at the spot where he had dug produced a deception of the eye, the result, probably, of heat and shadow and his own fatigue. For it looked as though the patch of turned soil undulated with a long, slow motion, like the tide upon a dark and alien sea.

He reached Isling shortly before eight o'clock, slung his bag in the hack, and took a seat. From the speed with which they raced south toward Westmor, he guessed that the driver during his absence had not missed a single superstition. Graham wore a faint smile. This was not the first time that he had observed how well the power of legend acted as a safeguard for secrets.

Darkness had nearly fallen and a few thin stars began to appear when they reached the Westmor station. After a moment's reflection, Graham decided to allow himself the luxury of a private compartment in order that he might study his prize on the return trip, safe from curiosity and questioning by strangers.

He had time enough for cheese and a draught of ale before his train was due. The ale refreshed him more than the light meal. A second draught brought him a sense of relaxation and a tingle the more pleasant because the dryness in his throat disappeared.

He boarded his train. The wheels moved and began to click until they made a steady, rhythmic beat, unexpectedly soothing; as the train pulled out of the station, Graham stared absently through the window, his thoughts far removed on the mystery that obsessed his life. He remembered the unhappy love affair that had originally driven him to the remote corners of the world; and how his successive explorations among remains of antiquity had furnished him not with an adequate substitute but an altogether different kind of passion. Atlantis, Lemuria, Chichen Itza, Angkor-Wat, the Sphinx, Stonehenge, Easter Island, the sunken cities off the coast of north Africa, and the great golden Dial of Nyamba—they were magic names that brought a quicker beat to his heart. Colossal monuments, giant statues! In what tremendous hands lay their origin? Did the dynasties that fashioned them leave their aftermath in lore of ages to come, the ogres of old fairytales? And why had their builders vanished into oblivion, so that no trace of them existed? Riddles—inexplicable riddles. They had tantalized him from the day when he first adopted archaeology as his hobby and profession, his life and desire; and they had continued to thwart him in spite of his subsequent researches into folklore, anthropology, and all ruins of the remote past. Sometimes he had imagined himself near a solution, as he believed he now might be. But granting his possible discovery of an answer, would he have advanced much further than before? Each step backward into prior eras necessitated another step, until the hunter lost himself in a labyrinth of origins and prime causes, or perished on the perfect secret, the beginning of life itself.

Rousing himself from the torpor into which he had sunk, Graham unlocked his bag and took out the image. As he unwrapped it, he vividly recollected the afternoon's events: saw himself digging around his first find, felt again that later frightful sensation of hanging above empty space. And, undiminished, his former distaste returned when he held the icon in his bare hands and watched its outline waver incessantly through change after eerie change. There was no accounting for it. Did it possess a hypnotic power which resulted in optical illusions? Or was he a victim of hallucinations, from eyestrain and overwork? He doubted whether this last guess had any truth, for his nerves had always been good; as to the former, it might contain an element of truth. The image compelled attention, and he knew that auto-hypnotism could frequently be induced by intently focussing one's eyes on a specific object. But this formed merely a possible, not a positive, explanation. He remembered the paradoxical postulates of Einsteinian mathematics, nor could he forget the visible testimony of his own gaze when he had witnessed geometry go askew and a solid body become a plane or—he hesitated over the thought—vanish momentarily from time and space. Graham sighed. This line of speculation led to another possibility: if the slab was not subject to the ordinary laws of physics, why could not the statuette also be an exception, since both were composed of the same material?

Graham examined the greenish surface in perplexity. It did not look like metal. It did not feel like stone.

It had the slippery texture of mica or soapstone, the hardness of quartz, the weight of gold, the fluidity of quicksilver—he abandoned the useless search for comparisons. The queer substance possessed that baffling quality of suggesting relationship to many known metals and rocks, but of preserving its unique difference. He observed that the blow of his pick had not made a mark on that tough surface.

He finally gave up his attempt at identification. That would be a task for chemists and physicists and laboratory analysis.

He continued his scrutiny of the object, to determine its use or purpose or function, until it dawned on him with growing irritation that he did not even know the precise appearance of the thing! Sometimes it seemed to be a pudgy, toad-like monster, then it resembled some primitive deity, or suggested an even more primordial entity; and in its final phase, it passed beyond anything he knew but somehow projected itself into a titan towering to the stars. Queer, this impression of giantism, and queerer still, the uncanny way in which the little beast gave a semblance of bloating out to enormous size. If only it would stop that infernal shimmering so that he could see it at rest for even one second! But incessantly its outline swam until Graham, becoming giddy from his effort to keep pace with each transformation, tore his eyes away. He felt a sudden urge to choke it until it squealed, to trample it beneath his feet, to hurl it through the window and watch it smash into a million bits. He knew he would not, for not only did the object possess a fascination of great power, it possessed also the attributes of a dynamo at rest. A physical force appeared ready to flow from it, an alien energy waiting only the proper authority or direction.

Completely baffled, Graham idly turned the image upside down. Its flat, circular base had a crust of hard earth on the bottom. The object, in spite of its small size, was of such massive weight that he could well understand how it must have compressed the soil if it had maintained its upright position over a great period of time. He scraped the crust away, pried and cut out flakes with his pocket knife. He had no worry about damaging the figurine. No man-made blade could affect it. He tested its hardness by a deliberate effort to make a tiny scratch, an effort that broke off his knife-tip.

But gradually, as the base became cleaned, his interest heightened; for there on the bottom, in clear, minute incisions, he beheld the same inscriptions and symbols which he had seen on the slab at Isling that very afternoon.

He pondered long over this new discovery. The hands that fashioned the slab must also have moulded the figurine. But what purpose lay behind those enigmatic writings? He wondered if he would ever decipher them, or grasp their significance. As it was, their incomprehensible nature added another question-mark to the mystery into which he steadily plunged deeper. Graham had never been a student of languages, and had no flair for them, but he was broadly familiar with the history of speech and writing. His own field of research had given him visual acquaintance with many written languages, ancient and modern. He could not read them, but he recognized texts in Sanskrit, Chinese, Egyptian hieroglyph.

Mayan pictograph, Arabic, old Greek, primitive Siamese. He searched his memory in vain. He could recall nothing like these characters, with their whorls and curves and serpentine twists. Were they the language of Atlantis? Or did they antedate all the tongues of earth? Whose hand or what race carved them?

And not only the characters baffled him, but the geometric symbols, like the shorthand for some super-Einsteinian system of mathematics that concerned multiple time and multiple space. In only one particular did Graham feel the least bit of understanding. Among the incisions lay two circles, each with a multitude of points in different arrangements. After long, close scrutiny through his pocket magnifying glass, he was convinced that one circle contained a map of the stars according to their present position. The other circle must also be an astronomical chart, but if so, it presented the heavens in such an unfamiliar array that he could not comprehend it. Perhaps it depicted some other segment of the universe. Perhaps it showed the same stars as the first chart, and at the same time, but from the totally different perspective of an observer in another galaxy. Perhaps it dealt not with space, but time—the same stars of the first chart as they were astronomical eons ago, or would be in far, future eons.

With a feeling of frustration, he wrapped the image and replaced it in the bag.

His watch indicated twenty minutes before eleven. Not quite an hour's journey remained. Graham settled himself in his seat and brooded on the events of the day.

Click-click, click-click, click-click.

He shifted himself into an easier position and with a determined effort turned his thoughts aside from the whole affair. Perhaps it would be well to study the image in further detail at the Museum, for days if necessary, before returning to Isling. Photomicrographs of the incredibly small, etched lines would help.

Click-click, click-click, click-click.

The rhythmic sound of wheels and the swaying motion of the train had a soothing effect. His brain and body needed rest. He welcomed the approaching pleasure of bed and a good sleep.

Click-click, click-click, click-click.

His eyes closed, his head nodded, and he drifted toward the borderlands of sleep. . . .

With an abrupt start, he sat up, uncertainly awake. He glanced at his watch, which showed a minute past eleven. His nap had been short, fifteen minutes at most. Something had awakened him. He looked around the compartment, and peered through the window, but saw nothing unusual. Yet a feeling of unease persisted.

He listened to the noises of the train, and more distant noises that came dimly through the murk. Probably another electrical storm was brewing. He hoped he'd reach his quarters before he got caught in a deluge.

The distant sound came again. Graham strained his ears to catch it; was it really thunder, or the beat of his heart, or something else that existed only within his compartment? He strove to concentrate his attention. Faint and scarcely audible at first, the sound grew louder. Could it be a voice crying across the moors in darkness, rasping inhuman and foreign syllables? Did it come from outside, or from within, from the depths of his bag?

"*N'ga n'ga rhthl'g clretl ust s g'lgggar septhulchu nyrcg s thargoth k'tuhl s brogg meargoth s bh'rw'lutl ubwcthughu dägoth—*"

Not a word or syllable of that jargon held any meaning for Graham. The deep tone grew louder, it beat through him in waves, it excited and exalted him, it depressed and frightened him, with a force that he had never experienced. The windows rattled, the air vibrated with great beating waves of sound, he felt buffeted as in a hurricane. He covered his ears but the syllables surged through him, invisible tides, already at crest, but reaching higher. From everywhere poured oceans of unbearable sound that overwhelmed him in the bursting of new forces.

There was darkness in the compartment, and cold, and a vastness that towered beyond conception, and communion with the utmost abysms of time and space. There was a terror indefinable, of pitted surfaces that mushroomed into thin emptiness between stars. A grayish-green flux enveloped him.

A woman's shrill scream anticipated disaster. Graham pitched forward as the brakes burned. The floor buckled and jumped at the ceiling. His bag bounced. In his effort to clutch it, he clutched emptiness. The bag burst through the window. Graham lurched in a final effort to seize the bag, lurched into a mantle of velvet, a cushion of darkness and absolute quiet.

III

MISSING: A GOD

GRAHAM opened his eyes to a white cot. He smelled the odor of antiseptics. Sledge-hammers throbbed in his brain.

He had difficulty thinking. A hospital. A wreck. A train trip. A green image. A graveyard at Isling. And sounds in the night.

He tried to sit up. The effort sent a wave of nausea over him and he fell back, his face drawn. The sledge-hammers beat louder. He raised an arm feebly and found a bandage on his head.

For what seemed an age he lay very quiet until his headache became more bearable.

Here, under the influence of hospital surroundings, the adventure seemed unreal, remote; but it must have been only too real, he reflected grimly, or he would not have wakened with head bandaged. Perhaps it was fortunate for him that he regained consciousness at all. As for the image, when he had recovered he would open his bag and—

Memory returned with a shock. He had last seen the bag crashing through a compartment window. And with it went the fantastic figurine. If it were lost—No, that could not be, the bag must have been found near him in the wreckage. It was unthinkable that he should be thwarted after he had made his most important discovery.

He painfully turned on his side and surveyed the small room, even peering under his bed at the expense of another agonizing headache. There was no trace of the bag. He sank back, plunged into gloom, wondering whether his trouble had been wasted, or worse still, whether he might not have been a victim of mind mirage.

But was it necessary to consider the bag lost? He sought for some more satisfying explanation of its absence. Possibly it had been picked up by the rescuers and handed to the proper authorities. Or it might be awaiting him now in the hospital's checkroom. Graham's spirits rose. Of course, there existed the chance that the missing bag had been crushed by debris, a catastrophe which he decided against; the likelihood seemed small that anything short of irresistible force could damage an idol with such peculiar properties and so impregnable to the blow of a pick. At any rate, it served no purpose to worry over the whereabouts of the bag until he could talk to someone who knew the facts.

His thoughts next pivoted around the nightmare just prior to the train wreck. The shadowy and ill-defined events kept intruding into the stream of consciousness. Interesting in its own right as a pure hallucination, with the bizarrerie of a dream-world, the menace in green blended and symbolized the happenings of the previous day. The sequence had certain elements that puzzled him, and whose meaning eluded his grasp. Perhaps he was over-emphasizing its importance, but he felt instinctively that it contained significant warnings or hints—if he could find them.

The sledge-hammers began to pound louder once more.

Graham sighed. He sometimes found it an effort to think, but how much greater the effort not to think!

He estimated he had been conscious for at least fifteen minutes, since it seemed like hours. He raised himself cautiously again to see if he could reach the service-bell without another wave of nausea. He managed to press the button, though fiery lancers dueled in his brain. After a few minutes a nurse entered. She possessed a plain, cheerful face, and tawny blonde hair the color of taffy. Nature had assembled her lavishly. She bore an impressive superstructure and an equally prominent extension in the opposite direction; assets and attributes that over-balanced her, coming and going, but not without attraction of a massive kind.

Graham mused, "Outstanding examples of developments that are both steatopygous and mammosus."

"I beg your pardon?"

"The Greeks and the Romans had words. The Anglo-Saxon equivalents, while pungent, are less esthetic."

The nurse looked blank. "Did you ring?"

"No, the bell did," he responded with a trace of brusqueness. He hated superfluous questions, especially those of feminine origin.

She smiled like a tooth-paste ad at his unexpected reply and retorted, "If I were to answer in kind, I'd say that Sir Warren left a piece of his own mind, such as it is, in you."

"Sir Warren?"

"Yes, the surgeon, Gifford. He operated on you yesterday for skull fracture and concussion of the brain. A minor operation, of course."

Graham said, amused, "I deserved that. I'm glad you said it."

He digested her bit of information slowly. Gifford, a noted brain specialist, was an acquaintance of some years standing; he had made several contributions to the displays and exhibits at the Museum.

Graham asked, "Where am I? And how long have I been here?"

"Middletown Hospital, Room 713, since early yesterday morning. They brought you in shortly after the wreck and operated a few hours later."

"Was there a brown, medium-sized bag among my belongings?"

"I don't know, but I can find out."

"Will you, now? It is a matter of great importance to me. If it would not inconvenience you."

The nurse turned with a majestic sweep of her clearances fore and aft, and left the room.

She was not absent for long. When she returned she said, "No, your bag isn't here. The desk says that nothing of yours is listed. You were an emergency case with only the clothes you wore."

"I was afraid of that. How long will I be here?"

"A week, at least."

He remained silent after this new blow to his hopes. A week! By that time, whatever slight chance he now had of regaining his bag would have completely vanished. He determined to leave the hospital, with or without permission, long before a week had passed.

The nurse looked at her watch, then busied herself a few seconds with bottles and glasses.

"Drink this." She handed him the results of her work.

He swallowed the mixture. The sledge-hammers faded away. The nurse went out the door. He began to drift into a realm where islands of remarkable shape floated on a sea by cliffs with astonishing slopes.

He awakened in late afternoon to find Sir Warren at his bedside. Graham promptly gave him urgent reasons why he must leave the hospital at the earliest moment. To his surprise, the surgeon said he could depart in a couple of days; the operation had covered only a small area. Graham would need to avoid any blow or bump on the head until the cut bone had knitted and the skin stitches had healed.

"The quick operation relieved the pressure," Gifford said. "What may cause trouble later is the concussion. The effects may not become apparent for months or years, in the form of headaches, dizzy spells, impairment of vision, or even tumors. But we've done all we can for the present. If your work is so important, you can leave, at your own risk, of course. But don't overexert."

The intervening time dragged slowly. Graham passed it chiefly in planning his next actions, and in ransacking his memory for some explanation of the phenomena he had witnessed. He dredged up data from the buried knowledge of years, yet came always to blind alleys and dead ends. Recovering the lost statuette became a mania, an obsession. Therein lay mystery that dwarfed the archaeological riddles he had encountered at prior times, and mystery it would remain unless the icon came to light again. As for that cyclopean presence that had bulked around his compartment—did it bear any relation to the image?

For once in his life, he regretted a lack of intimate friends in whom he could confide. He had always run free of the pack, and if he talked to acquaintances about his experience he knew only too well the certain result: "Poor old Graham. Sad case, isn't it? And he did seem to be doing such good work. But that's what usually happens, over-work and then a breakdown."

During part of his forced leisure, Graham tried hard to recall the uncouth syllables he had heard just before the wreck. "N'ga n'ga. . . . clretl ust s g'lgggar septhulchu. . . . thargoth. . . ." What did they mean? They neither sounded nor, when he wrote them down, looked like any language he had seen. Another riddle to investigate.

Maze upon maze since the idol had first emerged from earth! Of only one matter was he sure: he had been dropped into the labyrinth, he would explore all avenues for the way out. The game lay in the pursuit, regardless of whether he ever caught up with his quarry.

Modern techniques accomplished a minor miracle that a preceding generation could not have performed in a month. Graham, with a bandage taped under his hat, left the hospital eager to resume his quest. A total of four priceless days had been wasted.

He first stopped at a back-number newsstand and bought copies of all papers since the wreck. He read the accounts in detail, scanning also the lost and found ads and the personal notices.

A paragraph in one of the early reports puzzled him. "The cause of the disaster which killed nineteen and in-jured fifty-seven is as yet unknown. Testimony of witnesses indicates that the track was clear, no rails being loose or spikes pulled. The engineer, who died shortly after the wreck, could offer no explanation. He declared that, proceeding according to schedule, he was on a straightaway at approximately fifty miles per hour when a terrific tug broke the train into two sections. The front half jumped the rails, then ploughed along the roadbed for a few hundred yards, before the cars sprawled around the locomotive. The fourth car of the nine-car train was flattened by some freak, as if a great weight had dropped upon it. Eleven bodies were removed from the fourth car, its occupants save one having been instantly killed. The rear part of the train piled up around the fourth car. The lone survivor of the demolished fourth car, the curator of the Ludbury Museum, received a fractured skull and lies in serious condition at Middleton Hospital."

Later accounts added nothing new. Fresher news already crowded them from the front page—a shipwreck in the Atlantic. Graham had had enough of disaster and wasted no time on the story. But nowhere could be find mention of the missing bag.

He discarded all the papers except three. He hailed a taxi and drove to his quarters. From there he telephoned all the dailies and ordered the following notice inserted in both the personal and lost columns for a week. "Fifty pounds reward for the return of a brown bag or for its contents; initials C.E.G.; lost in train wreck at Nottington."

He next called an automobile renting agency and requested delivery of a good sedan. Promptly on its arrival he paid the deposit guarantee, settled himself in the seat with a package beside him, and drove off.

Threading his path at what seemed a turtle's gait through streets and suburbs to the west, he stepped on the accelerator and drove furiously as soon as he reached more open roads. In little more than an hour he came to the scene of the wreck. He parked the auto on the roadside and walked across some two hundred yards of meadows to the railroad tracks.

The rails had already been repaired and the debris removed. Graham had small hope of finding his bag but he intended to check every detail in his efforts to regain it.

He walked along the tracks for a half-mile, scanning the ditches and fields. He criss-crossed the grass and weeds until not a yard of ground or clump of trees or depression had been overlooked. He found a great assortment of objects—sandwich wrappers, rusty bolts, bottles, tins, beer caps, a dead cat, paper cups, cigarette and cigar butts, chewing gum foil, a tattered scarf, the usual accumulation along railroad tracks. And nothing else.

He returned to his automobile and continued on his way, heading now for Isling.

He stopped briefly for lunch. He arrived at Isling in early afternoon and drove straight for the Vadia and the Devil's Graveyard. Near the spot where he had entered several days earlier, he parked the automobile. He carried the package with him.

He walked to the small mound of dirt that marked his previous excavation. It lay undisturbed, he judged after prolonged scrutiny.

He commenced digging leisurely, and with frequent pauses for rest. His head throbbed with a dull ache. The soil was still loose as he had left it. He therefore made much rapid progress than before as he steadily went deeper. He anticipated the sound of steel striking the unknown substance, and each pebble he hit made his heart beat faster momentarily.

When he finally heard the sound he expected, he had reached bottom where the great green block lay. He rested for several minutes under the spell of disappointment, before he could bring himself to accept his failure with a measure of resignation. Not a trace of the missing image had he found.

His secondary purpose, at any rate, could be accomplished. With infinite pains, and prepared for a scramble to safety at the first sign of danger, he continued removing the last handfuls of soil until he had laid bare the surface with its inscription. Opening the package he had brought, he lifted from it a bottle of white powder which he dusted over the surface. He blew away loose flecks. The powder filled the carved lines and, white against the greenish background, made the inscription stand out boldly.

He next removed a camera and bulbs from the package. He took several flashlight exposures of the inscription. His task finished, he gingerly climbed back to the rim of the hole, expecting the gulf to open beneath him at any moment. He uttered a breath of nervous relief when his feet were back on reliable ground. Eventually, he planned to investigate whatever lay beneath the green block, but for the present he had other matters to attend to.

Night had fallen by the time he returned to the city. He left his films with one of the museum staff who possessed a dark room with complete equipment, and who promised both contact prints and enlargements by nine o'clock the next morning.

Though weary from his trip and labors, Graham had not yet finished. After dining at his usual restaurant, he returned to his quarters and until late in the night sat at his desk poring over data, notes, diaries, memoranda, and miscellaneous records of his past work.

The following morning, as he examined the photographs, he felt satisfied by their perfect clarity. Not a detail had turned fuzzy even in the enlargements. Since nothing had so far developed from his newspaper insertions, he felt convinced that his best chance of progress now lay in attempting to decipher the symbols.

This might prove a task of utmost difficulty; and if not hopeless, at least a matter of months or years unless he could find some shortcut in the form of a clue or key. How could those queer whorls and unfamiliar loops be read by anyone except their author, let alone be pronounced? Where could a start be made in translation?

The instant the thought of pronunciation occurred to him, Graham had a hunch. The voice he had heard in his compartment—that queer, harsh discord of consonants and breathings like no other language he had ever heard—could it have a bearing on or relationship to the etched symbols?

He went to the telephone and made a call. "Hello. Professor Alton? This is Graham speaking. Could I make an appointment with you this morning? . . . Yes, it's rather important, something that I'm sure will interest you deeply. It pertains to an inscription whose writing isn't like anything else I know. I've not the least notion of its origin.

I wouldn't even promise that it's related to any known language, living or dead. . . . At eleven? Good. I'll be there."

Graham rang off. Alton would have invited a tramp in at three o'clock in the morning if he spoke a dialect or jargon new to him. If anyone could decipher the writing, Alton was the man. A famous philologist and student of languages, he had made history in the field of creative scholarship with his elaborate work on the Polynesian tongues and his pathfinding commentary on the translation of Mayan pictograph. Graham knew him well, for Alton was sure to visit the Museum whenever an ancient frieze or artifact or statue with any kind of inscription became added to the permanent collection. Alton was at present laboring on a comparative study of African dialects which had an oral tradition but which had never existed in written form.

At the appointed hour, Graham met Alton in his office at the University. He laid out the photographs, and placed beside them a sheet with letters in block print containing as much as he had been able to remember of the alien utterances he had heard in the train compartment.

Alton peered through his thick-lensed glasses for a long study of the photographs. Finally he asked, "Where is the original?"

"At Isling, not far from Stonehenge."

"At Isling?" Alton sounded surprised.

"Yes, I took the photographs myself. Here is what I think may be an approximate pronunciation of some of the symbols."

Alton studied the lines of Graham's block printing with

a frown of concentration, his lips moving as they silently formed the words and phrases. He muttered audibly, "Hmmmm. Before Sanskrit. And a modification of the Ulonga chant. Yet the two together. Here. In England of all places."

Alton looked up. "Will you leave these? I think I may be able to do something with them. I won't promise a complete translation, but we shall see, we shall see. I will need to consult some recordings I made in Africa a few years ago." His voice ceased. He forgot that Graham was present. He became wrapped in study of the photographs.

Graham left. For the first time he felt that he had begun to make progress. If Alton failed him, he would very likely have come to the end of the trail—the dead end. And if the missing image were not found, he would have a riddle never to be solved, unless the green slab opened a way to new approaches or disclosed something that would throw light on the phenomena. But Alton's researches in comparative languages had been so outstanding that Graham believed he would achieve at least partial success.

On returning to his rooms, he telephoned the newspapers. No information about the bag had come in reply to his advertisements. He resumed his examination of his notes and files. He decided to add to them the clippings about the train wreck, and accordingly spread out the three newspapers he had bought that morning.

The first yielded a complete story with pictures and graphic descriptions of the accident. The second contained a résumé, further small details, and theories advanced as to the probable cause. But a newer headline dominated the front page of the third and most recent paper, an account of a missing ship. He looked at it idly, until a phrase caught his eye, "—greenish cloud enveloping the ship as the tramp freighter *Rawlins* passed it about midnight—"

Graham quickly ran his glance down the alphabetical list of passengers, but recognized only a couple of the names. ". . . Farrell, Dan . . . Marsh, Joane . . ."

He went back to read the main despatch from the beginning.

IV

THE HAUNTING

DAN FARRELL staggered to his feet and looked around him in a daze. What had happened? He heard a crackle ahead, the hiss of escaping steam. He saw the glare of fire, while moans and cries filled the night. He didn't seem to be physically injured. He must have been tossed free through the open window by some freak of the wreck, and knocked out cold. A man lay near him, with head crushed. Farther away a girl's arm rested by a mass of crumpled steel, bright red polish on her nails; the girl's body must be lying elsewhere. Dan could not identify another sprawled heap as man or woman. He heard the sound of automobile brakes. Headlights burned on the road a couple of hundred yards away. Figures with kits hurried to the wreck. Ambulances waited with doors open. A procession of men with stretchers crossed the field.

Dan had no desire to help in the rescue work. He wanted to get away, and fast. His ship was scheduled to depart at noon. He had to catch that boat. Dan believed he had a wide margin of safety, but he did not intend to run any needless risks. If he did not use his passage, it would be days before another swift liner left. He had tried in vain to buy an air ticket. The earliest plane reservation he could make lay weeks ahead.

If events developed according to plan, several days would

elapse before they found her body. More time would pass while they tried to establish her identity. He expected his handiwork to present them with a very difficult problem. And the toughest part of their investigation would lie in trying to find any connection between the murdered woman and Dan Farrell. Dan felt quite sure that his name would never enter the case. But if by some unlucky accident the authorities wanted to question him, he intended long before then to have reached at least the middle of the United States.

He wondered what hour it was. The accident had smashed the crystal of his watch and broken the hands off. By the number of people collecting at the scene, the doctors and ambulances, he judged that he lay unconscious for perhaps an hour.

He looked at the wrecked coach longingly. All his clothing lay in two suitcases buried under sheared and flattened steel. He doubted that any recognizable part of them would ever be recovered. However, the suitcases contained no documents, initials, or identification of any kind, and he regretted their loss solely because of the inconvenience. His funds were ample to make necessary replacements.

Dan walked along the ditch, paying little attention to where his feet took him so long as the general direction proved away from the wreck. He stumbled over something and fell across the object in his way. It was a medium size bag that might easily pass for a doctor's kit.

Dan picked up the bag. It felt heavy for its size, but it would serve a double purpose. It ought to be useful in escaping from his immediate surroundings, and it would also replace his own luggage. He'd look more natural boarding the ship.

He passed several running men who flung questions at him but he mumbled his replies. Stretchers went by him, some empty, some full. In one of them a man with graying hair lay unconscious, an emergency bandage on his head. Dan thought it looked like the fellow he'd talked to at the Ludbury Museum a couple of weeks earlier, but he couldn't be positive in the darkness.

Ambulances and automobiles were parked along the road. He examined each as he hurried on. Several of them contained the ignition keys. He chose a late model that resembled a doctor's car. With a quick glance around to make sure no one stood near, he climbed in and turned the ignition on, putting his bag on the seat beside him.

He drove off, satisfied he had not been observed. Under the circumstances, he might have a half-hour or more before the owner missed his car. And additional time would pass before the authorities could be notified and an alarm given for the stolen automobile.

But in less than an hour Dan had reached the outskirts of London. He abandoned the vehicle on a deserted street. Taking the bag, he walked around the nearest corner and strode toward the lights of a main thoroughfare. He hailed a taxi and told the driver to continue on the same street until he recognized his destination.

Several times during the next hour, he changed taxis, walking for blocks between fares, until he felt certain he had made it virtually hopeless for him to be traced.

Once, after he first entered the city, he went into a railway station to brush up his appearance by the mirrors of the lavatory. Towards dawn, he ate a good breakfast including shredded wheat with sliced banana and cream, bacon and eggs, fried potatoes, toast with marmalade, fruit salad, and three cups of black coffee.

He bought all the morning papers. A sense of relief came over him when he found no reference to the discovery of any murdered woman's body.

Dan took the train to Southampton. There he bought the items he needed most urgently: razor and blades, a shaving bowl, brush, after-shave lotion, talc, toothbrush and paste, bath soap, shirts, ties, underwear, and socks, handkerchiefs, pajamas, a lounging robe and slippers, and a wrist watch. He also bought a couple of bottles of Scotch to celebrate; and a valise to hold everything. He could have put the small bag he was still carrying in the new piece of luggage, but he liked the appearance of things better with two bags.

An hour before scheduled departure, he crossed the gangplank. The *Western Queen* was the newest of her kind, a single-class luxury liner not even half the tonnage of the huge old queens of the Atlantic. She had never yet required four days for the crossing.

He let a steward carry his bags to his stateroom. Then he went on deck, restless till the vessel would get under way.

It did not appear to him as if the ship would carry a capacity passenger list. The homeward flow of American tourists would not reach full tide till later in August. Judging by the rate at which passengers embarked, he guessed that perhaps two-thirds or three-fourths of the berths would be occupied. He might be lucky enough to have the cabin all to himself.

While he stood at a rail aft, he looked idly at other passengers in the vicinity. One of them, a woman, was glancing toward him at the same instant.

Something stirred in Dan, something deep and strong that made him take a pack of cigarettes from his pocket and light one. He inhaled hard, before looking at the woman again. She was still appraising him.

She might be, he thought, perhaps twenty-five or six. She had a firm, supple body, and a curious way of lounging off balance against the rail. It reminded him of the casual ease of a tigress that could afford to slouch because it could spring so swiftly. Her mouth, with its sensuous lips, held a cruel quirk in the corner. Her face was beautifully made up, though it was an interesting rather than beautiful face, tanned a golden brown, of delicate texture. Her nose was graceful, but her eyes set wide and her cheekbones high. Her eyes were a light, smoky blue that bothered him. She wore a summer dress of some gray material, very simple, very effective, very smart, with a necklace of gold in hollow square links. But her hair made her outstanding. It was silky and soft and luxuriant. It was glossy white on her left side, mixed of silver and black in the middle, and a lustrous black on the right. It made her look old and young. It divided her as though she were two different women. She wore it shoulder length in a straight cascade on the white side, with the tips curled under in a ring; but the dark side had a wave down across the forehead to a careless toss behind the ear.

That hair fascinated Dan. He had never seen anything quite like it.

He threw his cigarette away and walked over to her, deliberately, while her gaze held his with equal fixity. Dan said, "It's startling. It's none of my business, but is it real?"

"Thank you. It just grew that way."

Even her voice bothered him. Low and vibrant, it carried a sort of suppressed intensity, as if it emerged through a web of restraints. She had a lovely throat. It reminded him of someone else's, though the other throat was altered now, and lay where sunlight never came.

Her voice drifted into his thoughts. "Is something wrong? A spot of dirt, perhaps?"

"No." He raised his eyes. "Just admiring your necklace. You wear it well. Gold is attractive with that hair of white and black."

She smiled. "For a man who needs a shave, you're very polite." The smile brought warmth to her mouth, and her lips, in subtle change, became far more tempting.

"I had a hard night," he said. "The name is Dan Farrell."

"I'm Joane Marsh."

"Traveling alone?"

"Yes."

"Married?"

She hesitated, before saying, "I don't know."

Her reply proved so unexpected that it left Dan speechless for several seconds while he tried to think of some appropriate remark.

She came to his rescue. "Did that surprise you?"

"Well, most women seem to know whether they're married or not."

She nodded. "You're an American?"

"Yes. I've only been here a month on—business."

"That explains it, then. Why you didn't recognize my name. Joane Marsh—and Thomas Marsh."

Dan, puzzled, wrinkled his brows slightly. "I'm sorry to say, it doesn't ring any bells with me."

Joane said, "I was an American, too. I met Tom when he went to New York on business several years ago. I came to England and married him three years ago. He was moderately well off, owned a famous old cutlery factory in Sheffield, and a rather large country estate. About a year ago, he disappeared."

"I've heard of cases like it. Cigarette?"

"Thank you." He lighted it for her, and another for himself. She turned her head a little to blow the smoke away from him. "He disappeared the night before he was scheduled to make a business trip to Paris. I offered a reward of five hundred pounds for any information that led to finding him, or discovering his body. His company offered another five hundred pounds. The rewards are still standing."

"Amnesia, perhaps?"

She shrugged. "No one knows. The police of England and France made investigations. The papers were full of it for days. The authorities even combed the grounds of our estate, and I had them drag the pond to make sure he hadn't somehow met with an accident. But not a trace of him has been found. Oh, there've been the usual number of false reports. But nobody knows what happened. Maybe he was killed by a hit and run driver who hid the body. Maybe he fell a victim to amnesia and met death later under some other name. Maybe he's still alive. Perhaps he hated business or being tied to a home, and made careful plans to break away.

"As I say, I don't know what happened. It's been a hard year on me, living alone at first, under suspicion, doing no entertaining, having no social life. Recently our friends have begun to accept the fact that he may never be seen again, and to be more sympathetic toward me. I felt I could take a long trip. I needed it. And now—you."

Dan looked blank. "Me?"

She turned her face full towards him, her head tilted back, the smoky hue of her eyes as live and as dangerous as the surge of electricity he had once seen leap from anode to cathode at a power display. The impact of this restless new force in her came to him as a tangible wave. He saw almost a hunger in her expression.

"Yes, Dan. You remind me of him. You're the same height as Tom, I come up to your shoulders. You have the same kind of rumpled brown hair, the same sort of face that's pleasant and yet has an underlying hardness or singleness of purpose when it needs to, the same weight— a hundred seventy?"

"Sixty-five," said Dan. "Close enough." He flipped his cigarette over the rail. "How about cocktails before dinner? I'm going to shave and clean up now. Say five o'clock?"

"I'd love it, Dan. Why don't you call for me at my stateroom when you're ready?"

"All right, Joane, I'll be there at five."

"It's number thirty-seven."

"We're neighbors. I'm in fifty-nine. Don't worry too

much about the past. Whether he's dead or an amnesia victim or dropped out of sight intentionally, he tied your life in a knot. I don't see that you owe anything more. To me you're just—Joane."

She spoke lightly but her eyes were thoughtful. "That's what you get for asking people if they're married—they are and they aren't."

"They aren't. I'll be looking forward to cocktails."

Dan left her at the rail and went to his room. He did not glance back.

After shaving, he took a shampoo and hot shower. While soaping himself he heard the blast of the ship's whistle, followed by the first sway of motion. He felt much better.

His spirits rose further when he dried off and entered the cabin. No other luggage had been brought in. Cleansed and relaxed by the shower, he became aware of his great tiredness. He stretched out on the lower berth, completely relaxed. The voyage had begun well. The face of Joane and her wonderful hair kept floating into his mind. She was an unusual woman, both in her story and her exotic appearance. Her face floated away from him. He followed it and slept.

When he awoke, his new watch indicated a quarter after five. He'd probably have slept on except that he felt hungry. He hadn't eaten since breakfast. He dressed in haste. He'd be late for his appointment with Joane. His feet touched the small bag. He wondered what it contained, but he had no time to look now.

At half-past five, he knocked on the door of stateroom thirty-seven.

Her muffled voice answered, "Come in, Dan."

He entered. The living-room alone was larger than his cabin. Costly furnishings decorated it, from mahogany table, writing desk, and overstuffed chairs to console radio and sofa. Joane was not here. He went on through an open door. The bedroom had a full-size bed, also of mahogany, with a cover spread in rose brocade. He saw a mahogany bureau, and a dressing-table or vanity with triple mirror. The furniture, all of modern design, looked expensive and swank. The bedroom contained even an ample closet, door ajar, with a row of dresses, suits, and coats.

Several pieces of luggage lay on the floor, of fine leather and styling, crisp and new, with the monogram "J.M." burned in charcoal black against leather the hue of ripe corn kernels, a matched set. A handbag of alligator hide rested by a party dress, a dinner suit, a negligee robe, and a nightgown draped over the foot of the bed.

Joane loved the good things of life, and could afford them, he thought.

From the partly opened door of the bathroom her voice called, "Dan?"

"Yes."

"I'm not quite ready yet. Sorry to keep you waiting but I just finished a shower. I won't be long."

"Take your time. There's no hurry."

He turned, relieved that he did not need to apologize for his tardiness. Before he could take a step, her voice came again. "Dan, would you mind looking in my handbag? I think I left my lipstick there."

"I'll see."

He searched among a compact, keys, some currency, a handkerchief, a solid gold cigarette case with matching lighter, a newspaper clipping. The clipping, folded and worn, carried an account of the missing Thomas Marsh. It added nothing to the story she had told, and had evidently been published shortly after his disappearance. Dan noticed a description of the missing man, and a reference to an accompanying picture; but the clipping did not include the photograph. He wondered why she had not kept it. Searching through other items in the bag, he located the lipstick and called, "It's here all right."

"Would you hand it to me, please?"

As he started toward the shower room, a buzzing began, rose to a loud, sharp note, then died out.

Joane stood by the wash basin, facing the mirror, her left arm raised. She wore a short slip of satiny white from waist to knee. Her legs were attractively moulded, with the sheerest silk hose he had ever seen. He liked the contour from calf to ankle. Underneath that startlingly contrasted hair which hung to her shoulders, the tan of her face flowed down across the smooth and supple curve of her back to disappear below the line of the white slip. Her right hand awkwardly held a small electric razor.

Joane lowered her arm and half-turned. She said, "Thank you, my dear," in a voice that had a casual caress. She took the lipstick and placed it on the shelf over the basin, beside a make-up kit with creams and polishes and perfumes. She half-turned again, but in the opposite direction. Her breasts were of exceptional beauty, firm, with a slight upward tilt, so that they seemed larger and rounder at the base. The narrow areola around each nipple clung like the budding heart of a blood rose against the tan of her skin.

She handed him the razor and said, "I don't seem to be managing very well. I'm not used to this kind."

"You're doing all right."

He felt the deep surge again, like a cresting tide. To his careful study, the hollows looked flawless, but he flicked the razor dial and put it in motion. Her skin possessed a glowing warmth, a special vitality; and it gave off a faint perfume, from the body lotion she had used.

As he finished one side and turned to the other, revolving her gently by her shoulders, he saw at close range that surprising division of color in her hair. It was genuine and natural, beyond any doubt. The white on one side and the black on the other mingled strands a trifle left of center, but she had skilfully parted and combed them, so that a slight irregularity of line was imperceptible except to eyes as intent as his now were. The line did not follow straight, but curved to the right; from behind, the white overwhelmed the black.

Dan clicked the dial on the razor, after grooming the other perfect hollow. "Finished, I think."

She tested her fingers. "I couldn't have done as well."

"Anything more?"

"No, and thank you."

He laid the razor on the shelf. "That's a magnificent tan you have. You must know a good place."

"There's a clump of trees around an open bank of turf at the pond. I've been sun-bathing there all summer."

"Any white patches?" he asked, with a candid challenge.

Her eyes lifted to the mirror. "The voyage has only started."

Dan went out and through the bedroom. He took a cigarette and, after a few puffs, felt his pounding heart begin to quiet. Joane baffled him. He did not know what to make of her bizarre story, her direct methods, or her unexpected remarks. She violated the conventions. She destroyed the normal social customs of living. She displayed the calm acceptance of habit in her most outrageous reversals of usual actions and attitudes.

She came out wearing a short white jacket, open, over a salmon colored sweater of luxuriant wool in just the right thickness, since she plainly had not put on a brassiere, and a skirt that shimmered with midnight blue.

Dan glanced at her appreciatively. "I don't know which effect I like better—before or after."

"You don't know yet. So far it's all been—before."

The bar had begun to empty as passengers left for supper, but many a head turned when Joane went by. They found a table and Dan ordered double Scotch and sodas for two.

"It's late," he said. "We won't have much time before dinner. And I feel like celebrating."

"So do I. I'm beginning to wake up from a horrible nightmare. I'm glad I met you, Dan. It's the best thing that could have happened to me."

"You mean, without whiskers."

She smiled. "Well, you look ever so much better. You did need a shave."

And you didn't, he thought. But he merely said, "I don't

think you could possibly look better. The women are all green with jealousy and the men are all eager to know you. You're terrific as a lady-killer and man-killer."

The drinks came. Dan raised his glass. "Here's to the black and the white. By the way, does it carry through?"

She touched her glass to his. "That's a good question. Here's to finding the answer."

Dan drained his glass, and set it down. Her actions and answers always seemed a step ahead of him. Joane put her empty glass beside his at the same instant.

"Fast work," said Dan, and ordered from the steward. "Two more. Double Scotches."

Joane said, "I don't know how long I can keep even with you. That's the first drink I've had in over a year."

"Don't try to make up for lost time in a hurry."

"I want to. I want everything. All there is of everything. All at once. And lots more of the same."

He felt a tremor at the back of his neck, a creeping tension. She spoke with an earnestness and passion whose gathering power put him on guard, but at the same time attracted him intensely.

Dan observed, "After all, this is only the first day out."

"It's been a wonderful beginning."

He raised the second drink. "I hope the ending is better. Here's to a long night and a gay one."

She tilted her highball against his. "I hope it lasts for ever."

He noticed for the first time that she wore no rings. She had fingers that looked slender but strong, tapering with individual twists and turns between the joints to pointed nails that bore a polish like port wine. Interesting hands.

He took only half his drink. "For ever is too long. Make it, till we reach New York."

She leveled her glass to match his. "Are you stopping in New York?"

"Only long enough to catch a plane to Minneapolis."

"I've never been that far west. Do you live there?"

"It's the home office of my company. Flour milling. We have a large export business."

"Is that what brought you to England?"

"It was mostly business. I had some odds and ends, too, such as going to the Ludbury Museum to get the stuff they have about grinding and storing grain, and baking bread, in ancient Egypt. For a promotion we're doing on wheat and history."

"The Ludbury Museum? I've been there a couple of times with Tom. Did you meet the man in charge? Graham, I think his name was."

"Yes, he helped me with what I wanted."

"Rather a decent fellow though I don't think he paid much attention to women. That reminds me, you never told me if you were married."

"Not any more."

"You were once?"

Dan shrugged. "She ran off with another man. I got a divorce."

"You never saw her again?"

Dan sounded brusque. "Once. She wrote me a letter. I didn't like what she said. I didn't answer it, but I did see her."

"Has she changed any?"

"Considerably."

"Do you want her back, as she is now?"

A cold shiver swept through him. "Good God, no." He raised his glass. "That's all dead and buried. Let's forget the past. Let's be here and now."

"I feel those drinks already. I don't know what the rest of this will do to me and I don't care. Dan."

"What?"

"Just—Dan." Her eyelids rose a little as she touched her glass to his again, then slowly drew down till the pupils were half-hidden.

Dan finished his highball. He didn't feel happy. He didn't feel unhappy. He simply felt Joane. And Joane was a strange new force.

"Let's eat or we'll be too late. I missed lunch," he said. "Do you want to dress for supper?"

"I did, for you, but I won't. I'm beginning to be a bit dizzy."

As they walked past the bar, Dan said, "Mind if I have a quick one?"

"If you do, so will I."

"Maybe you can't take it after a year's lay-off."

"I'll take it."

He ordered the Scotch straight, with soda on the side. "Damned if I know what this one is for," he told her. "But darling, I hope it's good."

"I hope it's good and bad." Her words came in a sultry drawl.

He gazed at her uncertainly. "I don't get it."

"You will. Though I wished you wouldn't." That odd,

cruel smile had begun to hover in the corners of her mouth again. Perhaps he didn't mean cruel; rather, an enigmatic smile, of provocation, secret satisfaction, and deviltry. He considered her, her mouth highly seductive; just wide enough, with lips just full enough, and firm enough. It took a close look to detect the lipstick, skilfully applied, a subtle improvement on nature.

Dan gulped his drink. She sipped hers, swallowed, moistened her lips with slow enjoyment of the tip of her tongue, then drained her glass.

"The Scotches were heavenly, my dear. I liked them so much. Thank you."

They went on to the dining salon. Joane said very little during the meal, though twice Dan looked up to find her studying him with a warmth of pleasure in her expression, but a distant drift in her eyes. It was as though part of her radiated a welcome to encompass him, and part had gone a-wandering in fields afar.

He felt the impact of the highballs, in spite of the fruit cocktail, hors d'oeuvres, cream of fresh broccoli soup, the entree of planked flounder garnished with drawn butter and finely chopped parsley, the main course of T-bone steak charcoal broiled with mushrooms, flanked by shoe-string potatoes and stuffed baked tomato, together with combination salad bowl.

It was after meringue glacé and coffee, while letting cigarette smoke float gently from her lips, that Joane suddenly spoke. "I'm going to lie down for awhile. Till I don't feel quite so dizzy."

He accompanied her to her door. She walked with the same long, easy stride as before, almost seeming to flow down the passageway. He could detect no change except her quieter mood. "Are you sure you'll be all right?"

"Of course, my dear. Do you like to dance?"

"Sometimes. Would you care to go to the ballroom later? Dancing begins after nine, I believe."

"I'd love it. Call for me about nine-thirty."

"Something to look forward to, darling."

Dan returned to his own cabin. He was a trifle drowsy himself, from the dinner, the highballs, and his inadequate nap of the afternoon. He intended to stretch out for an hour or so.

As he entered his cabin, his glance fell on the bag. He had brought it a long way. He might as well examine it now, and see what kind of luck he'd had.

He placed it on the lower berth and opened it.

The pick, spade, and hammer stunned him. His hands shook as he lifted them out one at a time, and sent them through the porthole. "If that isn't the damnedest thing," he muttered softly. "I'd have thought they came back to haunt me, if they weren't so infernally real."

He went over to his new suitcase, beads of sweat on his forehead. He brought forth a bottle, opened it, and drank a deep swallow. He used a quarter-tumbler of water from the bathroom faucet as a chaser.

Dan returned to the bag, his nerves steadying. The remaining objects consisted of canteen, some tools, and a bundle wrapped in cloth. He removed the bundle, whose weight surprised him, and set it aside. He carried the bag to the porthole. By pushing and squeezing, he finally succeeded in shoving it through.

One more item, and he'd be finished with the bag and its

gruesome reminders. He unfolded the wraps of the bundle and lifted a greenish little object.

He must be getting dizzy again. He didn't seem quite able to see the thing clearly, or to grasp what it represented. Its outline wavered, as if it were changing into something else. And that gave him a peculiar unease, because he hadn't seen enough of its original shape to know what it changed from. It lay singularly alive in his hands, and emitted a tingling sensation, like some kind of invisible, radiant energy. It produced a shock-effect on him, for it possessed a hypnotic influence that absorbed his attention, yet it also manifested a quality of evil, of supernatural malignity.

Dan shuddered. He wrapped the cloth around the demoniac thing and walked to the porthole. But try as he might, he could not swing the bundle high enough to push it through. Sweat gathered on his forehead and trickled off his chin. The drinks must have drained his strength, or the sinister little imp weighed far more than he had suspected.

Breathing hard from his exertions, he abandoned the attempt after several minutes. He tucked the bundle under one arm, crossed the compartment, and went out.

Dan had almost arrived at the door to Joane's stateroom before he saw that it was open, and that she stood just inside, apparently debating some action. He had no wish to pause or to explain. "I'm in something of a hurry," he said. "An urgent errand."

She nodded silently. The bundle began slipping from under his arm, and as he grabbed for a firmer grip, the green statuette slid out of the cloth folds and dropped with a heavy thud. He flung the cloth over it and hastily picked it up. He hoped she hadn't seen it. He didn't look back. With a feeling of anger against the quivering thing in the cloth, he strode to the fore companionway and climbed to the promenade deck.

The night was clear and warm, a bright lemon moon hung high in the east, the sea lay nearly calm, and the *Western Queen* showed scarcely a roll. Dan hated the beauty of the night, the mild breeze, the damp, salt tang of the air. He hated them all because everywhere he turned, other passengers stood talking by the rail, smoking by the bridge, reclining in deck chairs, or strolling around. Dan didn't try to heave the bundle overboard, in the presence of others. He was afraid to try. He was afraid that he might not be able to succeed, and he didn't want to become a center of attraction.

He covered the promenade deck, the weather deck. He spent an hour prowling around lifeboats, smoke funnels, air vents, the bridge. Always he met travelers enjoying the view, an occasional crew member at work, or lonely souls off in obscure recesses.

Dan went below, still carrying his bundle.

Half-way to his cabin, he noticed a metal door over a fire hose. He opened it. Additional hose lay coiled inside. A quick glance around showed the passageway empty. He shoved the bundle under the coils of hose, closed the door, and went on.

Dan experienced a profound relief with that dreadful object off his hands. He was further relieved to find Joane's door also closed. He didn't want to see her now. He walked swiftly past stateroom number 37.

In his cabin, Dan gave way to the shakes. He poured a third of a tumbler of Scotch. He drank it in several degrees, sitting on the lower berth, until the turmoil within him began to undergo a soothing change. When the glass stood empty, he looked at his watch. It surprised him to find the time nearly ten o'clock.

He had told Joane he'd come for her about nine-thirty. He'd be late again, but it couldn't be helped. Anyway, she might not be ready herself. She could still be sleeping. And he needed a shower, a good, cold shower, to shake off the creeps.

Dan undressed slowly. He laid out a clean shirt and socks. He smoked a cigarette leisurely, and let the Scotch warm him further before he went into the shower room.

Though small and compact, it was adequate, even moderately attractive. Tiling of pearl gray and brick red, alternating in a checkerboard pattern, lined the sides to the deck overhead. They made an almost gay impression.

Dan left the door open. He didn't want the bath to steam up. As before, he turned the top two knobs, for fresh water. He wondered why the designers of ships installed the second pair, the salt water controls. He had never met anyone who used them. Salt water left a sticky feeling the one time he'd tried it, years ago, with the result that he'd had to take a fresh water shower immediately after, to wash away the salt water residue.

Dan adjusted the temperature to a coolness that verged on being cold, pleasantly stimulating, but not a scourge of needles of ice. His spirits started to rise until he grew almost light-hearted. He began to hum the tune of a song. He came to words he remembered, and sang them involuntarily, *Just the way you look tonight.*

He stopped humming, the pleasure gone from his face. The words had a depressing significance for him. The sound of splashing water lost its agreeable note. What imp of perversity had caused him to select that particular phrase among all the thousands of popular song lyrics?

He soaped his face and neck. Even the fragrance of the lather upset him. He'd asked the clerk in that store for a cake of the best bath soap. He hadn't paid much attention to what she wrapped up; he assumed its quality because of its high price. But, as he'd already learned earlier in the day, it bore the scent of carnation and left a faint perfume that lingered on his skin long after. He would not have minded the woodsy tang of pine, or spruce; but carnation was too sweet, too heavy; he'd always associated it with somber occasions, the flowers around sick rooms and caskets.

He worked up a rich lather on his chest and back, his stomach and thighs. He'd certainly be late. The thought made him hurry the soaping. He stepped under the direct shower, watching the bubbles stream away, enjoying the little fingers of running water.

"Tom," said a voice.

Dan froze. A chill raised a gooseflesh army along his forearms.

"Tom," said a voice.

Dan turned. For an instant the spray fell upon him with the rush of a mighty waterfall, but it must only be the pounding of his heart, the convulsive throb at his temples.

Joane stood in the doorway. An unholy ecstasy shone from her face. The blue of her eyes had acquired a glow, like the mysterious and infinite glimmer of stars. Moonlight lay in the cascade of pure white hair that tumbled to one shoulder, but the dark heart of night nestled in the waves of lustrous black flung indifferently over an ear to the other shoulder. Even now, in the paralysis of a horror he did not yet understand, he stared with fascination at the bewildering beauty, the absolute contrast, of that fantastic, two-tone hair.

She wore a nightgown of some heavy material, glossy white, in Empire fashion, with short puffed sleeves, a short waist, and a long, flowing line to the flat sandals on her feet. Her toenails were enamelled to match the red of her fingernails. The gown had a bodice, of open mesh, in a broad pattern like a fishnet. The bodice flaunted her breasts in a wanton and deliberate mockery of the otherwise chaste nightgown.

She held the image in her arms. It lay there, a blob of abominable green and indistinct form, fluctuating through the cycles of its changes, and emitting a phantom fire. She held it cradled between her breasts; and her nipples, erect and taut against the mesh, seemed to possess a life of their own, thrusting toward the eerie object.

"Tom." Her voice came in a tender whisper. "You don't mind standing under the water, do you? With the white rocks and the brown rocks around you. You didn't mind, the night I rolled you down to the pond, down and under, did you? And dived in, and pushed the barrel into the deep hole, and scooped sand and mud with my hands till the hole was covered. You didn't mind, did you?"

"I didn't mind," said Dan. He scarcely recognized that dry, husky echo as his own speech.

Her murmured words carried the magic of poetry. "I knew you didn't mind, as I lay beside the pond the rest of the summer, talking to you, sometimes. And in the winter when the fogs came. And through the summer days again. You don't miss them, do you? For summer and winter never come, where you stand under cool, dark water."

The mounting tension in Dan swelled to a pressure head of unbearable restraint. The impact of water became a compression that generated explosive force. He whirled, frantically spinning the knobs to stop the shower. He turned, but she was gone. He heard the outer door close. He reached for a towel and dried himself in a panic haste. By the violence of his actions, he strove to release the emotions that seethed in him. He felt on the verge of some vague, tremendous doom. Had she seen him hide the green object? Had she found it by intuition, or by dream-impulse from a source and in a way that he did not understand? Did she walk in her sleep? Had she killed her husband, or had she brooded over his disappearance until she had imagined a guilt of responsibility that was not hers?

He didn't know. He hadn't time to think. That dreadful green thing must go overboard, immediately, even though all the passengers were witness. He stepped into the bedroom slippers and ran to the berth. He grabbed the lounging robe and slid his arms into it. He pulled the cabin door open, hoping she still walked near. Only an empty passageway met his gaze.

He hurried to compartment 37. He knocked on the door but received no answer. The knob turned and the door opened to his push. He closed it and stood listening for a few moments, but heard no sound. How long had she been gone? Five minutes? He walked toward the bedroom.

The Empire nightgown hung over a chair. Joane lay in bed, a sheet drawn to her throat. Her eyes were closed, her features relaxed, but a hectic flush heightened the color of her complexion. Her hair spilled across the pillow, the two shades tousled together in drifts of black interlaced by skeins of angelic white. One arm rested at her side; the other folded across her stomach, the fingers loosely encircling the green figurine which nestled on her diaphragm. Dan marveled that she could bear a weight so heavy as the green object, yet it rose and fell in the slow rhythm of her breathing.

An indistinct murmur issued from her scarcely moving lips. Dan, straining to catch the words, could make nothing intelligible out of those queer sounds. "N'ga n'ga rhthl'g clr'tl ust s g'lgggar—." She uttered them like a chant, like an invocation. Dan thought that a stronger radiance enveloped the green object; it spun through its ceaseless cycle of change, but now, in some extraordinary manner, it suggested enormous expansion and contraction, a projection to far recesses of night. Did he hear, as from infinity, words of answer in the same weird chant? Syllables as impersonal as the sea and resounding as though echoed through measureless caverns of space?

Dan stepped slowly toward the sinister statuette. In the chaos of his thoughts, in the spell of this nightmare, in the nervequake of emotions that shattered him, he walked as a blind man, with his hand outstretched, dreading the touch of the malignant doll that erupted through the fluxes of its own fantastic life.

He forced himself to grasp the figurine.

Joane's eyes opened in narrow slits, haunted, haunting him. "Tom," she whispered. "You wouldn't."

He tried to seize the image. Fingers of fury dug into his wrist with a clamp of superhuman fixity. The idol slid off her stomach. He swung his free arm toward the green gnome, but some other arm caught his neck and toppled him. He fought pressures and storms and the dancing haze of deliriums and boiling turbulences.

Her eyes opened wider and wider, the upper lashes lifting higher. The flush on her face blossomed throughout her body in a quiver of flame. Her mouth crawled up to his, with a feverish, shaken kiss, a long kiss of complete helplessness. Her trembling became a convulsion that united with his in apocalyptic fusion.

A buzz from the far world cut through the blank and blanketing outward layers of stress to the core of perception. Dan partly raised himself to look. He said in a tone of wonder, "The electric razor. It's working. And it isn't connected." He turned his head again down to Joane, and saw that she held the figurine at her hip. He could not see it clearly for the tempo of its cycle had multiplied to blurring velocity. All things were distorted in the phantom vortex of green, the percussive waves of sound, and the sweep of flood-tides.

Her free hand suddenly raked his chest in a spasmic clawing. The pain stilled him. He watched the drops of blood fall upon her breasts.

"Dan," said Joane. "Oh Dan."

The freighter *Rawlins,* east bound for Plymouth, sighted the *Western Queen* near midnight. The second mate, chewing the butt of a cigar at the starboard rail, was the only witness. The liner, leagues away, diminished towards the moonlit west. A glowing greenish haze enveloped it mysteriously, a vortex like a waterspout without a cloud. For an instant radiance hung over the vessel, then the torrent of obscurity, then only a furious foaming of the sea.

V

UNDER THE GRAVEYARD

THE circumstances surrounding the disappearance of the *Western Queen* made it as noted a mystery of the sea as the fate of the *Cyclops*. Newspaper mention of the queer green cloud caught Graham's eye, and he guessed that the lost image had been aboard the vessel. After the train wreck his bag must have been confused with the luggage of someone else and accidentally carried to the ship.

And if the green idol had accompanied the *Western Queen*, it had probably perished with the ship. Or had it? As he recalled its imperviousness to blows and its amazing properties, he became convinced that while it brought doom in its wake, the idol itself remained untouched. Where was it now? At the bottom of the Atlantic? Or somewhere southwestward in the direction it had been travelling? It had returned to the Devil's Graveyard once; could it be there again?

Alton might have a report on the symbols in a day or two; even a partial translation would be of great value.

Graham thought of going through his old files for miscellaneous information stored away in diaries and notes. There were the commentaries on Stonehenge, Angkok, Easter Island, and the great Golden Dial of Nyamba. He also wanted to study many volumes in the Ludbury Mu-

seum's library; works on folklore and the remains of
antiquity; on tribal rites and religious ceremonies; on
superstitions, taboos, demonolatry, and magic. But his
logical course would be to resume his investigation where
it had been interrupted. While Alton tried to decipher the
inscription on the photograph, he himself would find out
what lay beneath the green slab at Isling.

Graham spent the rest of the afternoon on his prepara-
tions. He knew exactly what he needed, but assembling the
equipment required time.

He hesitated only over the selection of the two men
whose services would be necessary. He decided on Bjort
Liska, from the Ludbury Museum staff, a young archae-
ologist who had helped him on several of his explorations
through Great Britain; and his janitor's son Thomas, a
strong man, and dependable, though of less than average
mental development.

The trio set out for Isling the following morning, and
reached the Devil's Graveyard at noon. It was another
muggy day, with haze in the sky, and oppressive heat.

They lunched on sandwiches and coffee out of thermos
bottles which they had brought along.

"I never ate in a graveyard before," said Thomas, looking at the old headstones with curosity.

"There isn't a better place for meals," Liska reassured
him affably. "Nobody bothers you, and you can take as
long as you want. I'll never forget the time I was a medical
student for awhile, and one day in the dissecting laboratory
I absent-mindedly left a tongue sandwich lying on top of
a—"

Thomas interrupted him, shaking his head in disapproval. "I don't know how you fellows can do it. I wouldn't be able to eat."

"Oh, you get used to it. The human stomache doesn't care much what goes on outside."

"Mine does."

Graham stood up from the fallen tombstone on which he had been sitting. "I'll get started on the excavation. When you two are through eating, you can unload the equipment, if you will. No hurry. I'll be at least an hour digging."

In the stifling heat, Graham began shovelling the dirt up. He worked without haste, and paused often to dry his face with a handkerchief. Now and then he heard Liska talking to Thomas as they brought equipment from the light delivery truck he had rented.

When his spade struck the great block, he climbed from the hole. The winch had already been set up. He studied it carefully until satisfied that they had planted it firmly and with maximum safety. He tied the end of the rope around his waist.

"Don't leave any slack," he told Thomas. "There's a sort of door that I'm going to try to open. It has a trick lock. It's apt to open very suddenly and leave me dangling in air. I wouldn't want to fall any distance with a rope around my waist."

"Cut you in two," Thomas agreed with alacrity.

"I hope not," said Graham dryly.

"Righto. I'll take care of my end."

Graham clambered back into the hole and finished clearing away the dirt, until he had bared the great greenish block. He examined again, with a sense of awe, the mysterious writing on the mysterious tablet out of aeons of time.

He strove to recall exactly what he had previously done. Had he not run his fingertips over the top rows of characters and then across a group of those middle symbols? Yes, that was it. As identically as possible, he repeated the action, with a tightening of his throat. He traced lines of characters, continued through circles, pyramids, cubes, planes.

And the transformation occurred, unexplainable, ghostly, as though substance had dissolved into shadow before his eyes. There were no hinges, no signs of leverage, and absolutely no trace of the block he had been standing on a moment before. One second he stood on solid matter; the next instant he felt the tug of the rope as he dangled over emptiness. Below him blackness, a vast corridor plunging toward what subterranean regions and what unsuspected end?

What had become of the green slab? And how would he restore it if he wished to? Disappearing solids, planes that became arcs, cubes that vanished in pinpoint spheres, and now a staleness of long imprisoned air—Graham shivered as he called to Thomas.

He untied himself when he stood on earth again. He said to Liska, "The keystone is open. There's no telling what lies below. As I explained yesterday, there may be very serious risks involved. If you'd like to reconsider—"

Liska peered down the immense shaft. "I'm going along. This is the damnedest thing I've ever seen."

Together they fastened a large canvas bucket to the rope. The bucket, square in shape, and reinforced at the top and bottom edges, contained an inner platform for additional rigidity. Graham put several implements and useful articles into the bucket.

In his final instructions to Thomas, Graham said, "Whatever happens, just wait here. We may be gone for a long time, perhaps all afternoon if we discover anything really interesting. The main thing to remember is, don't try to come after us, no matter how long we're below. When we've reached bottom, you can set the rope in the safetycatch. When we're ready to come up, we'll pull the rope which will ring the signal-bell. Then you can start the motor going. The automatic winch will do the rest."

"Simple enough. Maybe I'll take a nap while you fellows are down there."

"Just so you stay in the vicinity," said Graham.

Standing on opposite sides of the bucket, Graham and Liska found that the rim reached almost chest high.

"Well," observed Liska cheerfully, "at least we aren't likely to fall out."

Thomas nodded. "Make an awful splash."

"Lower away," said Graham.

Walls of greenish gray slipped by, smooth, unbroken. Graham thought they looked similar to the unknown substance of the key slab, but perhaps in a less pure state. Who or what agency had constructed this vertical corridor, when and for what purpose?

The patch of light above them dwindled and contracted to a point. As blackness overtook them, they turned lanterns on. Graham continued to study the lining of the shaft. The more he pondered, the more puzzled he became. What possible reason had there been for building and sealing a perpendicular well of such dimensions? Why had it ever been made? Above all, and this perplexed him most, whence came the skill and the materials to construct such a masterpiece of engineering in those olden centuries when primitive tribes roamed through Wiltshire? For obviously this corridor antedated the Vadia, the Devil's Graveyard, Isling itself, and the regional records.

An exclamation from Liska brought hollow and muffled echoes from the walls. "Extraordinary!"

"What?"

"This well. We've dropped hundreds on hundreds of feet already and there's no sign of bottom. I've been flashing my light down. How do you account for it?"

"I don't." Graham hesitated before adding, "I thought at first that it might be a sacrificial well of some sort, like those mountain precipices in Peru and Mexico where the Incas and Aztecs hurled living human offerings to the gods."

"A curious old custom," said Liska, "and certainly a regrettable waste of virgins. How old do you suppose this is?"

"That depends. If the builders first made a pit in the ground, and then sank the shaft, it could be of recent origin. But if they built it at ground level, as I believe more likely, then all that surface dirt is the accumulation of centuries. And not merely dozens of centuries. Much older than Stonehenge. By hundreds of centuries. Perhaps thousands."

"Stonehenge," Liska mused. "The best estimate of its age is 1800 B.C., more or less. If this is older, there are more gaps in our knowledge of archaeology than I thought."

"There are more gaps in all knowledge than anyone realizes."

Graham watched the steady upward drift of walls, wondering if the winch held enough rope. It would be ironic if their descent ended at some midpoint of vacancy.

The air held a pleasant coolness, after the mugginess above ground. But the coolness also contained a musty quality, the dryness of a chamber sealed for ages. It reminded him of a tomb in Egypt he had once opened, except that the Egyptian tomb had retained a ghostly scent of spices and perfumes, of unguents and oils; whereas this atmosphere carried nothing redolent, only stagnation.

He heard another exclamation from Liska. Graham flashed his own light downward.

They approached the bottom of the shaft. The bottom? He saw whiteness and grayness, spherical shapes and objects like sticks. He saw also that the walls of the shaft had begun to expand. The bucket neared bottom in a great hemispheric cavern whose sides flowed away beyond reach of his beam. The white and the gray objects became larger and clearer. The canvas bucket came to rest.

Graham surveyed the site, awed by its eeriness. Everywhere lay skeletal remains, white, gray, brown, some intact, others blending or buried with earlier deposits. Eyesockets faced him, jaws with a permanent grin, legs and arms and ribs naked of any covering. Man and woman, adult and child, by hundreds, by thousands and thousands, their bones wasted here in slow dissolution until they should finally unite with the basic dust.

In spite of his scientific training, Graham experienced

a psychic unrest. The sombre mood that grips the living in the presence of human decay was not his to repulse. Whence came these immeasurable remains? Wherein lay the origin of so great a mass of human residue?

The nearest skeletons were those of modern man, any man, any woman, any child. Graham examined several before moving on to investigate the dimensions of the chamber.

He had taken only a few paces when Liska called, "Graham, look. Dozens and dozens of these."

Graham walked over to examine the object. Liska reverently held a skull, brown from age and disintegration. The lower jaw had completely gone, the left cheek bone and most of the facial structure had badly deteriorated, but the cranium remained in good preservation. Graham recognized it at once as a skull of Cro-Magnon man.

"They're everywhere," said Liska. "We'll have the finest collection of any museum in the world."

"Good work, and it's only the surface," said Graham absently. He went back across the great white mound, his feet slipping occasionally on a skull or crunching in debris, a rib or humerus or ulna. Liska had already dropped to his knees, with the fervor of a Magellan or Galileo.

Graham noticed that the accumulation completely obscured the original floor. Where the sides of the mound sloped to meet the walls, the ossuary conglomeration extended to a depth unknown upon whatever base or floor there might be.

Liska scooped away dust and bones with the loving care of a collector. He brought forth a skull which he carried to Graham. His newest find was a relic of Neanderthal man.

Graham joined Liska in digging. They laid aside the larger pieces or better preserved fragments. If the funerary mound had sufficient thickness, might there not be fossils of still earlier man? They dug almost recklessly after a while because of the abundance of their material. They could afford to waste fragments and pieces, to disregard specimens that crumbled, because they found more complete parts.

Here 'lay intact skeletons on the surface, and below them bones, teeth, skulls, in different states of preservation or decay. They found greenish stains, of oxidised copper; and sometimes a stone weapon or ornament; but all near the surface, for farther down the stains did not occur, nor the ornaments; only flints and eoliths and artifacts came to light. The stains indicated the bronze age, and their absence the stone age, of man.

As they worked into the mound, a parade of man's life on earth passed in recessive eras. Whole skeletons represented Cro-Magnon man. Under them lay remains of Neanderthal man with his lesser cranial content, and below these the Predmost race, and the Grimaldi race; behind them Heidelberg man and Eoanthropus or Piltdown man, in a variety of types, some of which had never previously been known. Tens of centuries rolled into hundreds, and thousands of centuries mounted by thousands, as they sifted through this great wastechamber of all the races and all the ages of man. Rhodesian man, Pithecanthropus Erectus, Peking man, Sivapithecus, and the offshoots between, the side races and branches and transition types that had died out after brief existences. Dawn man and the missing members of the genealogical tree showed up one after another. The skull bones became thicker, the brain capacity smaller, the head more beetling and apelike as they dug yet farther down. And then came the sub-men, Propliopithecus and Notharctus, the line from Miocene times backwards, until they finally approached strata of such powdery decay that not even guesswork could provide any clue to their age or nature. Five hundred thousand years they had burrowed into the past, and farther, how much farther they had no way of telling. More than a million years from the life of man was preserved in the successive layers and deposits which they had pierced. And when they at length ceased their labors from sheer fatigue, the awe in Graham's eyes reflected the wonder in Liska's.

How had so complete a fossil history of man accumulated here? What protecting hands had entombed and preserved these remnants of all the dead through abysses of time? What undreamed of power had built this monument and guarded it while continents emerged or disappeared, while glaciers crept out of the north, while earth buckled and mountains upheaved and the sea reclaimed portions of land, and the hills wore away in constant transfigurations and mutations which had altered the globe? That the chamber with its ancient bones, or the deep corridor with its verdigris colored walls, had a recent origin seemed unthinkable; yet no more difficult to accept than that such a subterranean vault could have withstood unchanged the enormous pressures and stresses and strains of earth during ages that defied comprehension, during gulfs of time that had watched the world formed and re-formed through incessantly changing aspect.

Graham felt tired. The maelstrom of mystery, instead of narrowing, swung wider and wider. The utter lack of answers or explanations, the futility of conjecture, and the addition of phenomenon to phenomenon, question upon question, wearied his mind.

He rose to his feet and selected a few of the finest specimens which he had laid aside. "Do you realize how long we've been here? Nearly three hours. We can take some of the skulls with us. There's enough to come back to for months."

"I suppose so," said Liska. "But it's a sort of fever that gets you. You don't even know that time passes when you strike a great find like this. We'll have something for all the museums in the world, but we'll make Ludbury the best."

A sudden frown of worry entered Graham's face. "What was that sound? Listen."

A gentle swishing came from the center of the cavern. He heard a faint rasping, and a sharp snap as a bone cracked.

He flashed his light toward the bucket.

The rope was falling in a jumble of coils that spilled across the bucket and spread over the bones.

VI

THE TIME TRAP

GRAHAM stared blankly at the collapsing rope until the end whipped across the ossuary pile. The hollow rustling died away. Skulls and bones which had lately seemed mere relics of decay began to acquire an aspect of malice. He imagined a kind of sardonic life in those grins and eyesockets. The cavern of the dead had become more than symbolic. Were their own skeletons to be added to these immemorial reliquiae?

He shook off his lethargy and strode toward the fallen coils.

"Looks like we're in a bit of a predicament," said Liska, worried. "Do you suppose the rope could somehow have dislodged the safety catch? If it did, it would fall of its own weight."

"It's possible," Graham answered. "It couldn't have happened by itself, but of course Thomas might have stumbled and knocked it loose by accident."

He picked up the end and examined it, a puzzled expression in his eyes.

"What do you make of it?" asked Liska.

"I can't account for it at all. It didn't slip off the winch. I'm sure of that."

"Could it have been cut?"

"It wasn't cut," Graham spoke positively, continuing to

study the loose end. "If a knife had slashed it, half or two-thirds of the strands would be level, and the rest frayed raggedly as the weight of the rope broke them. But this entire end is perfectly even, though slightly fuzzy."

Liska came to him and stared intently at the rope. "That's a queer one, all right. It doesn't look like either a cut or a natural break."

"It's rather as if each fiber snapped separately and at exactly the same place," Graham said, baffled.

"How could that happen?"

"There's not much use in speculating how it happened. Our chief problem is how to get out."

"That's just a matter of time." Liska sounded hopeful. "When Thomas sees what happened, he'll get the extra cable of rope out of the truck, put it on the winch, and lower it to us."

"We don't know what took place up there," Graham told him. "If Thomas met with an accident, he may not be able to help. And if it was anything serious enough to knock him unconscious, we could rot while waiting for a rescue that may never come. No, we'd better examine this entire chamber and see if there's some other way out."

"It sounds reasonable."

"We'll start from the wall nearest the spot where we were digging. Suppose you work along the wall to your left and I'll take the opposite way until we meet. There may be an opening somewhere—you know the signs to look for. Here are candles and matches."

Liska set out, minutely examining the walls, the remains underfoot, and even the arch of the ceiling a hundred feet overhead. Graham went in the opposite direction, until he gradually lost sight of Liska because of the curvature of the walls and the ossuary mound which prevented a direct cross view.

Graham kept a close watch for inscriptions or symbols, but the greenish surface was devoid of markings. He frequently tapped the wall, which invariably proved both solid and massive. He continued searching for a crack, opening, or aperture of any kind.

He felt a double responsibility in that he had persuaded Liska to accompany him, and blamed himself for the unfortunate accident that had imprisoned them. From time to time he sent his beam toward the bucket at the peak of the mound, in hope of seeing a new rope lowered by Thomas.

The tomb's atmosphere assumed a depressing influence; this enormous mass of earthly remains; the solitude that blighted; the idiot grin of lipless jaws, the stare of sockets that contained no eyes, and the talons of thin hands, all carried their own foreboding.

He had discovered nothing when he again caught sight of Liska as he worked his way around the chamber. Liska was kneeling.

Graham walked over to him. "Did you find something?"

"I don't know, but it looks promising. There's a sort of shallow area here where my feet sank a little and the debris seems looser, so I thought I'd dig down a ways. What success did you have?"

"None. Not a sign of an opening. A really disappointing failure."

"Why?"

"Because it would be something new, and distressing,

in my experience if there's no exit or entrance except the one we came down. Monuments of the ancients, like the oracles and mysteries, and especially those concerned with burial chambers, usually had more than one way out."

He dropped beside Liska and helped him exhume. The material did seem more loosely packed here than elsewhere. He scooped for a few minutes, then struck a match and held it close to the wall and as far down as he could reach. The match burned with a steady flame, unwavering.

"Not a sign of a draught," Liska fretted.

"Discouraging, but let's dig on."

They deepened the hole, heedless of the priceless remains that they tossed aside. The hole grew steadily larger, until Liska's hand slipped out of sight.

Liska said, "This is it."

Graham struck another match and held it at the opening. The flame did not flicker.

The relief that Liska had showed melted away. "On second thought, maybe this isn't it. The flame didn't move at all. And if there's no drift of air, that probably means a dead end ahead."

"I'm afraid so," Graham agreed.

They worked more carefully in order not to start a continuous avalanche of bones sliding down to block the entrance they were clearing. They could hear loose pieces occasionally slip along the slope below them. When the opening grew large enough for a man's body to pass, Graham squeezed as close to it as he could and sent his light flashing ahead.

The burial pile slanted sharply downward for perhaps a dozen yards, an incline of skulls and skeletal fragments and protruding deathsticks. It ended on the floor of a corridor that extended indefinitely beyond range of the light.

"There's the answer to one question," said Graham. "This mound we've been digging into is more than thirty feet deep at the center." He moved aside for Liska to examine the slope.

Liska whistled softly. "And the chamber—what would you estimate its diameter to be? A hundred yards? There must be tens of thousands of skeletons here altogether."

What enigmatic purpose had created this most gigantic of all mausoleums? Whither led the corridor that swept away like an imposing cathedral arch? What hands had constructed it in what forgotten vistas of time?

"Ready for a slide?" Liska broke in on Graham's reflections.

"Yes, but we ought to make the best of both chances."

"Of course." Liska thought it over. "One of us should stay here, in case Thomas sends another rope down. But I always did like to go after something new."

"And this is the reward." Graham glanced at the dark chamber. "Something new, something old."

"An accident. We can't help that."

"I don't want any more accidents, but if there are, I want them to happen only to me. We're at least in a position to hope, here. I expect nothing but trouble in that tunnel. Therefore I'll see where it leads."

"It may be a long walk," Liska warned.

"It may be a long wait," Graham observed.

Graham went to the canvas bucket and pulled the coils of rope aside. He wanted extra batteries and bulbs for his flashlight from the equipment. He peered at the shaft overhead, but saw nothing, and heard nothing.

He walked back to Liska. "You'll find food and canteens of water in the bucket. Plenty of matches, candles, cigarettes, flashlight bulbs and batteries, signal flares, and so on. If Thomas sends another rope down, go up. Go up immediately, then lower the rope again, in case I have to come back this way. Do that, and nothing more."

Graham climbed into the excavation at the base of the wall. He eased himself through the narrow opening, and slid down the mouldering incline. His last glance backward showed Liska in the glow of his flashlight, dimly shadowed and ghostly, with projecting bones and vestiges of earthly ruin strown thickly around him.

Graham reached the bottom and stood up. He turned his back on the vast burial mound. He brushed the dust from his clothing, dust as fine as talcum powder.

He faced a tunnel or conduit approximately five feet wide and ten feet high. As far as his beam extended, the tunnel stretched away in geometric perfection, the sides perpendicular and parallel, the slight arch overhead balanced by an equal but inverted arch underfoot. The same metallic greenish substance of the chamber lined the sides; and nowhere could he discern any trace of a joint, a block, a seam, a cement, a weld, or even a crack or flaw. The tunnel was an engineering marvel; it looked as though the builders had moulded or cast it in a single unit. It flowed into the blackness ahead with absolute straightness.

Near the edge of the ossuary heap, an impalpable dust lay thickly upon the inverted arch of the floor, but as

Graham began walking, the powdery silt thinned out until finally he trod on the clean surface of the tunnel. Nothing marred the dull, smooth polish; not a variation in the greenish hue, not a drop of moisture, never a fallen section or any sign of a break in the flawless symmetry.

Minutes mounted into hours as he walked through that tremendous corridor. His steps made a monotonous muffled sound that echoed hollowly from the walls. The beam which he flashed sent a small island of light moving between infinities of blackness; and his feet provided a faint shuffle that floated between dead silences. The beam divided a rhythmic retreat of blackness ahead from the encroachment of blackness behind. Save for his ghostly tread, the silence was sepulchral, as though he walked down the aisle of some deserted, illimitable cathedral.

He watched in vain for any rupture of the surrounding walls, or a side passage, or any deviation from the straight. The air hung still and dryly musty, except for the fitful stirs of his passing which gave the illusion of barely perceptible motion. Though stagnant, the atmosphere had lost the heavy mustiness of the huge wastechamber.

Time ceased to exist for Graham in the monotonous cadence of his steps, and the accompanying echoes that fleeted eerily among the flowing darknesses. He began to feel a haunting conviction that no matter what direction he walked, there would always be an endless obscurity ahead, that no matter how far he traveled he would never pierce the shroud.

At what point of his progress, or at what distance from the burial chamber, or even at what hour there came a change, he did not know. Contact with reality had vanished in this ageless corridor. He had entered the world of illusion and dream, where things that are not, are. And a transformation had occurred, of such subtle and gradual nature that he could not remember where it began. The blackness seemed less intense, the walls more distinct. He switched his flashlight off in order to dispel the illusion. Had his eyes finally adjusted to the deep gloom? Had his conscious mind drifted away into the realm of phantasy?

As far ahead as he could see, till the corridor plunged onward beyond the limits of vision, and as far behind, the walls, floor, ceiling, every particle of greenish surface, even the air itself, emitted a phosphorescent glow that emanated from no visible source, a sinister and awesome radiance. All things shone with cold, flowing flame, and luminous waves poured even from the arch above him. It seemed, also, as if the walls contracted and enlarged simultaneously, as if their dimensions underwent a geometrical realignment. The corridor swept onward for indefinite distances, yet dwindled to a point immediately ahead; and all around him it gave a semblance of swaying and collaspsing and expanding, an impression of rapid change and unstable flux. Absolute silence prevailed; and the close atmosphere remained undisturbed by motion; but the paradoxical unrest of solid matter continued incessantly.

The witnessed phantasmagoria became inseparable from figments of imagination under the impact of perceptions of the supernormal. He could not assimilate or classify a unique experience that bore no relation to any past experience. It destroyed the validity of his senses by taxing them with a totally new and different kind of reality that had no connection with the reality of the world he had previously known.

There were times when he walked straight ahead with as terrific difficulty as though he climbed a precipice; and there were times when he catapulted frantically forward as if he had fallen from a great height; but all the while the corridor plunged onward on its even course while ballooning and condensing through magnetic tensions. Had any system of mathematics permitted a horizontal plane to become a vertical solid without dimensions within the same plane and without deviating from the horizontal, this baffling circumstance might have been more easily comprehensible, but Graham wandered dazed through the violences of ultranatural experience. He had acquired the dull, automatic persistence of a drowning man who continues to struggle as he goes down. He advanced through an interminable nightmare where time prolonged itself upon itself; a vortex of impalpable flame, cold fire of a color unlike any color of earth, reeling miles down a sunken gallery of endless dimensions, floors that swam free in mushroomed space, mockery of lucent green surfaces that closed him in yet opened upon the borderlands to far immensities of hyper-regions beyond comprehension.

And still the drunken dance of walls and floor continued through oceans of frozen fire in expanding rings and contracting spirals and distorted ratios, pulse-beats of apocalyptic presence. In that maelstorm of alien forces he perceived vaguely the symbols of the keystone; and their cryptic lines, suspended against the phantoms of change, retreated and advanced in unison with the compression and multiplication of the corridor. Slipping, staggering, sliding across dimensions and into planes, Graham found himself before the symbols and flung his hands to embrace them as though they might prove to have substance in this drift through the realms of implacable unrest.

Floor and walls and ceiling interchanged. Spaces and curves and distances and geometry ran wild. The vertical became the horizontal, duration and extent and being merged in some other dimension that interlocked and enlarged them all. The luminous energy bathing the corridor with elfin witchfire in the color that had no name became the play of unimaginable powers surging into tortured vision. Dynamic vortices whirled where the walls had been, but the walls were there, and solid surfaces dissolved into opaque mist and radioactive cascades, the ceiling and the floor and the walls opened upon shimmering magnetic storms that streamed away in motes like the vanished cinders of stars.

VII

OUT OF STONEHENGE

GRAHAM heard a cricket chirping and opened his eyes to the night sky. He lay on the ground, breathing in the scent of grass and earth.

His body seemed a single throbbing bruise. His head ached. Even his mind felt bruised and blunted. He slowly got on his feet, wondering where he was.

Great shapes loomed around him. Huge sentinels of stone ringed him. Fallen monarchs merged with shadows, and masses of hewn boulders covered the ground.

These giants looked familiar, and Graham recognized them with dismay. He was in Stonehenge. At his very feet lay the altar-stone, farther away stood the lordly trilithons, outside them the inner ring of blue stones, and outermost of all, the circle of sarsens. Impressive remains of forgotten hands that had builded mysteriously for purposes beyond certain surmise, their enigma and the inscrutable testimony of their ranks had challenged conjecture over the centuries. But it was not the enduring riddle of Stonehenge that bewildered Graham and filled him with unease. He had emerged many miles from Isling. He could not hope to walk the distance back in less than several hours; he did not believe he could accomplish the task in his state of exhaustion.

He began moving past the gargantuan ruins and set out across the Salisbury plain. He walked for more than half an hour before he came to the first house with lights. The owner did indeed possess a car, though a small one; and upon the transfer of two pounds, Graham bought a ride to Isling.

The fatigue and aches lessened somewhat as he relaxed on the trip. The driver proved to be a taciturn man not given to unnecessary words. Graham preferred the silence.

His journey through the corridor had already begun to lose sharpness in memory, like a fading dream. He speculated about the happenings at the hazy and uncertain climax. Probably the keystone to the tunnel, similar to the keystone to the chamber, lay close by one of the relics at Stonehenge; with the inscription on both the inside and outside surfaces. He could investigate that possibility at some later period; his only immediate concern was the rescue of Liska.

Graham thought that he must have pressed the symbols toward the end of his journey through the corridor, and that the unblocking of the corridor had catapulted him to the world he knew. Perhaps he had simply walked through to the outside and collapsed from the shock. The entrance to the corridor must lie near one of the monuments, perhaps a trilithon or the altar-stone itself.

Past Isling, and on the Vadia approaching the Devil's Graveyard, Graham saw the outline of the truck still standing by the hawthorn hedge at the entrance. The rim of the moon had begun to rise, and the shape of things crept forth between shadow and light.

He thanked his silent acquaintance who promptly

turned the bantam automobile around and sped away.

Graham stretched himself. The trip had not lasted long, scarcely a half-hour, but long enough for his legs to become cramped in the midget car.

As he entered the graveyard he saw a figure sprawled on the ground near the winch. With instant alarm, he hurried over to it, for the figure lay motionless. But as he knelt beside it, his fears evaporated. Thomas was not dead or unconscious or even injured. He merely slept, with his head cradled face down on a forearm.

Graham shook him, and Thomas rolled over, blinking.

"What happened?" Graham asked.

"Huh? Oh, nothing much. I just waited around for a couple of hours or so. It was good and warm. I guess I fell asleep. Are you ready to leave?"

Graham ran to the winch. A length of rope still coiled around it, passed through the safety catch, and hung down the excavation. Deeply perplexed, he turned his flashlight toward the shaft.

The great green slab lay there. The rope dangled in its middle. So that was it, he thought. The keystone had returned to position. And in doing so, in the weird actions of its own geometry, it had occupied a section of space through which the rope passed. It had destroyed that much of the rope, severing it, consuming it, probably in a flash of destruction, if Thomas had been awake to witness.

But what had caused the keystone to materialize, to occupy its original place? And the question brought an answer. The answer seemed so obvious to him now that he considered it pure stupidity on his part not to have anticipated it in his plans. The keystone was a time-lock; if you knew the combination, it opened; and after a specific interval, it closed. This characteristic of it explained why he had narrowly escaped on the first occasion when he uncovered the slab; he had turned the lock by pressing the inscriptions, but before it could open he had closed it immediately by touching the symbols again.

Graham tried to recall how long he and Liska had explored the chamber before the rope fell. Approximately three hours, he judged. His estimate fitted in with Thomas's remark that he'd fallen asleep after a couple of hours, when nothing unusual had happened.

The time-lock was set, apparently, for a period of about three hours. It would open only when activated, whether the intervals between activation lasted for days, years, or millenniums; but once activated, it would close in three hours. He could open the lock again and bring Liska up, with an ample allowance for safety and accident. There would be at least a couple of hours to spare.

The astonished voice of Thomas broke his chain of thought. Thomas had awakened a little more. "How did you get back up?"

"Underground passage," said Graham. "The rope broke. We separated and I found a way out. Liska's still down there."

"Is anything the matter with him?"

"No. I ran into a little trouble, but he's all right. He can't be very happy, though."

"What caused the break? That was a new piece of rope."

"Even the best of ropes have been known to break. I'll need the extra cable off the truck. Can you handle it?"

"Sure, I'm strong." Thomas ambled away.

Graham tied the end of the remaining coil of rope on the winch around his waist, measured a length sufficient to reach the green slab, and locked the safety-catch. He let himself down into the excavation and traced the pattern of the inscriptions. Again the strange metamorphosis occurred, the stone or metal dissolving in a way baffling to behold, as though it whirled and tired and thinned and was gone. Again he hung over that great well, and gingerly hauled himself out of the pit, his feet braced against the slope of the excavation, sending little runnels of dirt cascading into the depths as he climbed to the surface.

Thomas rolled the extra cable drum of rope across the Graveyard and together they wound it on the winch. In twenty minutes Graham was ready for the descent.

"Stay at the winch," he told Thomas. "I don't expect to be down any longer than is necessary to fasten the canvas bucket and pick up Liska."

"I'll be glad to get away from this place myself. It's kind of spooky."

The voice faded as the walls began flowing upward. Graham had taken a flashlight from the truck and put an extra one in his pocket. He kept a tight grip on the case as he flashed the beam on the walls and into the void below. The absence of the canvas bucket made a profound difference in his sensations. It had afforded a feeling of security, deceptive, perhaps, and yet a tangible comfort. Now, as he drifted down with only the rope to hold him, he thought of a spider he had once watched as it lowered itself from a ceiling, spinning down and down on a filament of cobweb.

The walls flowed upward with a measureless and soothing monotony. He found it an effort to keep his faculties alert.

He thought of Thomas slumbering while great forces had been in action near him. Perhaps it was best that Thomas had seen nothing. If he had been looking into the excavation when the green keystone materialized in place again, with the rope dangling to its middle, he would probably have lost his head. At the least he'd have run off in a panic. And at best he might have sounded an alarm bringing forth the whole village, and perhaps authorities from London. All in all, Graham felt that Thomas had handled the situation with perfect tact and absolute efficiency. By falling asleep he had witnessed nothing, had felt no unease, had created no disturbance, and was therefore now in a position to give the most useful service.

At last the regularity of upward flowing walls came to an end. The sides curved away to the spaciousness of the ossuary chamber. He began swinging the beam of his flashlight. The great mound of dead appeared faintly in the far mist of the light, and floated toward him with increasing clarity. Even before he dropped upon it, he called, "Liska!" The name reverberated, in cavernous echoes, but no voice answered his.

He untied the rope, and for the first time began to feel uneasy about Liska. He stood for a few seconds looking around, sweeping the chamber with his light.

"Liska!" he called again. "Liska! It's Graham—where are you? Liska!"

Liska was thrown from side to side in decrescendo and whispered back and forth to die away in hollow little darknesses beyond reach of his light.

The canvas bucket and the coils of fallen rope lay near him. The equipment had not been disturbed, nor the extra flashlights and batteries touched.

Graham grew more uneasy and puzzled. He had begun to think that Liska must have gone off to explore the long corridor. If Liska had, Graham would face the necessity of following him, of making that same tremendous pilgrimage again. Though the hours of walking would be arduous, he could force his weary body through the toil. But the prospect of passing a second time through the supernatural buffeting at the end of the fantastic corridor daunted him. And if he had to undertake the strange journey, the time-trap would certainly close as before; but now Thomas would observe the phenomena, with results wholly unpredictable. In the effort to find Liska, Graham would leave Thomas exposed to a force with which he could not cope.

The flashlight began to slide in his fingers. He shifted it to the other hand and dried his sweating palm on his hip. And yet, he reflected, Liska, with all his experience, would not have gone wandering through a tunnel of unknown length without taking an extra flashlight. Liska had not waited in the chamber; but the evidence suggested that he had not set off through the corridor. Graham's perplexity grew.

Abruptly he strode toward the burrow that he and Liska had dug to the corridor. The rubble under his feet made dull crunches; the silences whispered.

He slid down the chute-like opening to the stately aisle, and threw his light as far as the darkness would yield. He saw only the greenish walls, mysterious and remote. Graham examined the edge of the debris that spilled to the floor from the mound behind. He saw nothing to show that anyone else had followed him. His beam showed his own dusty footprints leading away and thinning quickly until even they were imperceptible on the floor of the tunnel.

Graham returned to the ossuary cavern and began to examine the surface of the pile methodically. He swung the beam of his light from the fringe of the mound at the curving green wall to the apex at the center, his eyes searching and probing the measureless rubble. It had occurred to him that Liska might have discovered another corridor, and in the task of excavating, buried himself under an avalanche of debris.

He had worked his way around more than half of the mound, when his beam reflected the metal case of Liska's flashlight lying on the slope behind the canvas bucket. He walked toward it, and all at once his own beam wavered, and he stopped to dry his sweating palms.

For long minutes he remained in a kind of timeless trance, attempting to accept the evidence of his eyes. The shock was too great to produce action; it stunned him into a sad and regretful daze.

Beside the flashlight lay a few other objects: a belt buckle; a wrist watch; some keys and coins; an automatic pencil; shoenails; a pocket knife; buttons; a zipper—all those metallic and inorganic things that a man ordinarily carries in his pockets, or which he wears as part of his clothing. But of clothing there was none; just the tokens and mementos, scattered around a fresh skeleton that had not been there when he and Liska had first entered the chamber.

Many fragments of thought and bits of perception poured in a confused jumbled through Graham's head before he could sort them into a pattern for understanding and action.

Liska must have died instantly, like those thousands before him in the time-trap; at some definite but short interval after the trap closed, a force of great but unknown kind literally stripped the victim of life, flesh, clothing, everything organic. Graham reasoned that since the time-trap had an existence of about three hours before it closed, a similar interval of about three hours passed before the victim met death. It had taken Graham approximately three hours, from the moment the rope fell on him and Liska, to the moment when he reached the end of the corridor. Indeed, he now believed that those terrifying powers at work when he made his escape from the corridor were the direct cause of Liska's death, and that he himself had been on the verge of the same complete destruction and disintegration when he opened the exit at Stonehenge.

Liska had therefore become the first victim of the time-trap in thousands upon thousands of years. For Graham believed that the great green seal on the vertical well had originally been set at ground level; it was built to attract the curiosity and investigation of any man who chanced upon it, to become a sacrificial well for any superstitious tribe that lived near it. Then the Ice Age had come, and the detritus left when the glacier retreated had covered the slab many feet deep. He remembered that geologists differed in dating the period of glaciation. Estimates ranged from 40,000 to more than 1,000,000 years ago. But the formation of skeletons in the great pile indicated the Ice

Age had been relatively recent; so that the time-trap must have originated more than a million years ago; before the dawn of man; or, and this thought disturbed him deeply, at the dawn of human life; as though the time-trap had an intentional, deliberate, and calculated relationship to the existence of man upon earth. And to the removal of men from earth—random men, whatever men chanced upon the time-trap.

Graham walked to the canvas bucket with the slowness of fatigue. He took a length of the protective cloths that he had brought for wrapping any great or sizeable discovery, and gathered up the remains of Liska, together with the miscellaneous objects. When he had placed the burden in the bucket, he tied the rope securely, and signalled to Thomas.

As the slow ascent began, he thought grimly of other unpleasant hours ahead. It would be necessary to see the local authorities, to explain as much as he knew concerning Liska's fate. By then, the time-lock would have closed. If the authorities wished to investigate, to try to find the secret of the green slab, they were welcome to act. He doubted whether the inhabitants of Isling would exert themselves. Graham himself had no intention of ever again opening the seal of the time-lock.

VIII

"WHAT WAS IT THAT I SAW?"

BACK in his quarters, Graham awakened late the following afternoon. Long, heavy slumber had done much to refresh him, and now, after he had prepared a belated breakfast, he examined papers and mail. One thick envelope looked important. He tore an end off and drew out a single written sheet and a second envelope. The sheet contained a short note:

> 6, Hammervil Ct.,
> London, W.C., 1,
> 7th Aug.

My Dear Professor Graham:

The inclosed envelope was found in the desk of the late Professor Charles Alton. He apparently had just addressed it when he met with a fatal accident. Should you desire further particulars, you may communicate with me at the above address. I remain, etc.,

JAMES MARTEN, *Sec'y.*

The second envelope was addressed in a shaky, ill-formed scrawl that had none of the beauty, neatness, and legibility characteristic of Alton's handwriting.

He slit open the envelope and drew out several handwritten sheets. The early script was loose and rapid, the lines steadily became thinner and more weakly shaped as the letter drew to a close.

After his quick appraisal, Graham began to read carefully, pausing often to decipher doubtful words.

A dead man writes to you. When you receive this letter, I shall have joined that vast throng the recorded symbols of whose existence I have devoted my life to translating. These are my own final characters, for which there is no more fitting recipient than you, from whom this result had its unintended cause. My heart informs me truly that my time is ended. I am content, since one must be content with fate, though I could have wished for a fuller understanding of this occurrence. I have tried to reach you by telephone, but your absence has made it, I fear, impossible to speak with you again as I had planned. My hours are not many. I am thus compelled to write. I hope that I shall have sufficient time to write fully.

In simple truth, I believe that no other man alive could have successfully coped with the inscription which you requested me to decipher. This is no credit to me. I merely happen to have pursued special researches in fields which other scholars with equal or greater training had not examined.

As much for fear, then, that my labors on this final problem may be lost, as for hope that you can shed light on the fatal accident attending my work, I am sending you these results, imperfect perhaps, surely uncertain. Since I feel that you are engaged on an enterprise of danger, if my injury is to be regarded as indicative, I am all the more anxious that you receive the information you requested.

As you know, I have spent a large part of my life in other parts of the world. My interest in languages, both living and extinct, has carried me to many far places, and on ventures from which, not unlike Jason, I returned bringing golden fleece of a different kind. These researches into the origins and growth of languages have included for subject matter all peoples, all countries, all centuries. I fell far short of complete knowledge of man's varied symbols, the dream that I should like to have achieved, but I attained a familiarity with every known spoken or written language, and a mastery of some of them. I have also, in that part of my work which I prize most highly, recorded one hitherto unknown tongue and one forgotten language. It is these two that now assume a new importance.

About fifteen years ago, I accompanied the Richter-Angley expedition. Assembling at Hyderabad, we went north toward Chitral, our real starting point. From there we took a difficult route over the Hindu Kush Mountains, across the Pamir Plateau, onward to the Altai Mountains, and then eastward through the Desert of Gobi to Peking. Our purpose was to search for traces of early man in the region often referred to as the cradle of mankind.

We had extraordinarily good fortune almost at the outset. Approximately one hundred and fifty miles north of Chitral in wild country we stumbled on the ruins of a lost sanctuary or temple. There we made our first major discovery: a few mouldy parchment leaves, all that remained of a once bulky manuscript. These leaves were covered with characters rather like Sanskrit, but of vastly greater antiquity. Their resemblance to Sanskrit was analogous to that of Anglo-Saxon to contemporary English.

I named this forgotten language *Kanja* after the site in which we found the fragments. Eventually, working backwards from Sanskrit, identifying roots and stems, guessing when analysis and synthesis failed me, I evolved a translation, an attempt at reconstructing its grammatical basis, and a hypothetical pronunciation. You may have seen my published monograph, *The Kanja Fragments, Edited, Translated, and with Notes on Their Relation to Sanskrit.* The pieces themselves were of a religious nature and comprised fragments of a ritual; but I shall omit a detailed explanation of their content since it has no particular bearing here.

Years later, I was a member of another party which went into the Dark Continent; and from Africa came the second of my discoveries, the unrecorded Ulonga dialect. I was then collecting material for my still incomplete comparative study of primitive African tongues. In that region where Abyssinia, Uganda, and the Soudan are adjacent, I made my find and obtained several automatic recordings. I shall never finish the study begun then, or publish the results of my work; yet it was not wasted effort, for those records gave me the first key toward solving your inscription.

Without your written impression of sounds you had heard I might have got nowhere, or at least have been months at the task. As it is, I have been able to accomplish much in this short time. But the results have provided a new perplexity, and now my life draws to its close before I can ever contend with or hope to understand a fascinating and remarkable maze of linguistics.

These were my materials: the Kanja fragments; the Ulonga dialect; the Isling inscription; the phrases you had written as a possible pronunciation. I should like to know where you heard the phrases, and how you found the inscription, and the meaning of these separate links to some enigmatic chain. I can not know. The moving finger writes. But regrets are useless and the time for guessing is ended, so far as my life is concerned.

The materials cited offered me a choice from two plans of procedure. I could work backward from the Kanja fragments to the Isling inscription as I had worked backward from Sanskrit to the Kanja fragments, identifying stems, roots, and so on, until I should have a translation of the message. This was a logical and systematic method. It was also one of slow results. Or I could begin with your phrases, compare them with Ulonga, and compare these in turn with the Isling fragment. This was a much faster method, but also subject to greater error. I chose it, however, because of your urgent request. For the sake of accuracy, I intended to use the alternative method later at my own leisure.

My task was immeasurably simplified by your key words. *N'ga n'ga clretl ust s glgggar* bore a striking resemblance to the Ulonga chant which begins *'Nya 'Nya ke re telus tse gul ge ge gar,* and so on. The numerous but minor differences in pronunciation were easily accounted for as a natural modification of the original during ages of oral transmission. It was more surprising that the variations were not greater, since the Ulonga territory is thousands of miles from here, and from India; and since both the Kanja fragments and the Isling inscription must belong to a much earlier period in the history of man.

But to continue, your half-dozen words were a clear indication that what you heard was the Ulonga chant, or rather the pure, original form of it. If your words truly indicated how to pronounce the Isling inscription, then the Ulonga chant might conceivably be the spoken counterpart of the entire inscription. Now, since I already knew what the Ulonga chant signified, I would then have both the approximate oral sound and the translation of the Isling inscription. And, finally, I would have the written symbols for the Ulonga chant which had hitherto existed only as an oral speech for which no written language existed.

Having progressed thus far, it would be a simple matter to

re-establish the exact pronunciation of the entire inscription. I could accomplish this in two ways: by modifying the Ulonga chant along the lines that your key words indicated; or by assigning the key-words to their corresponding written symbols on the inscription, substituting oral sound wherever these characters re-occurred, and filling in the gaps by reference to the Ulonga chant. I made use of both methods before I was through.

I suppose all this may sound very confusing and muddled to you, but it was really a systematic and basic procedure. I began with your key words, *N'ga n'ga clretl ust* and so on. These resembled the Ulonga chant, *'Nya 'Nya ke re telus* and so on. Your key words were the oral equivalent of the Isling inscription. Therefore the Ulonga chant was a complete but modified pronunciation of the entire inscription. I re-established the original sound more accurately by revising the chant along the lines shown by your key words. And since I already knew the meaning of the Ulonga chant, I knew also the meaning of the Isling inscription.

That is to say, I knew its English equivalent, for I am not at all sure of its meaning. Tribal memory has here preserved a ritual through generation after generation from remote ages, though its origin and purpose have been utterly lost. There may be significance in the fact that the Ulonga bucks, no matter at what time of day or night they chanted the ritual, invariably faced eastward, and upward.

I am failing fast. My minutes are fewer. You will find my reconstructed pronunciation of the glyphics, and their English equivalent, appended, together with your photograph. The fatal accident which I mentioned earlier is rapidly overcoming me. I refer to it only because it seems related in some supernormal way to your problem.

About two hours ago, I completed the preliminary drafts

of my work. I read the Isling inscription aloud in an effort to voice its uncouth and almost unpronounceable phrases. As the last syllable fell from my lips, at the half-way mark of the inscription, a dead silence ensued. Suddenly the atmosphere became strangely electric. I felt keyed up, but thought my tenseness was a result of long concentration. And next I believed I must be on the verge of a nervous breakdown, for I seemed to hear as from infinite distances a repetition of those very sounds that I had just spoken. Or was it a delusion? I do not know, Graham, I shall never know. There was a vast guttural voice rumbling the unknown language, an approach of hideous noise, a cacophony beyond description. The walls of my library became as mist that bridged infinite space. I saw a fluid greenish palpitation around me and felt the pressures of unimaginable power. I reacted with such violence that I hit my head on a corner of the mantel and fainted.

When my senses returned, I felt nauseated and extremely weak. A pool of blood enveloped me. The shock and the loss of blood from the gash in my head can have only one result.

A profound depression dominates me. Vague blurs of places I know not and things of which I have no comprehension drift through my thoughts. Perhaps it is madness. Perhaps it is the anodyne of death. And perhaps it is telepathic imagery implanted by a thinking entity different from life as we know it.

My thoughts wander. I am finding it harder to concentrate. But now I begin to understand how you knew the pronunciation of some of the Isling glyphics. Fate be with you on whatever mystery you are trying to solve, and may your destiny be more fortunate than mine.

What was it that I saw?

Here the letter came to an abrupt end. Graham could not have made out the signature if he had not known the handwriting. Shaken by this latest death, he slowly folded the pages and turned to examine Alton's translation.

The philologist as always had done scholarly work even though his time had been short. What Graham found was analogous to the Rosetta stone. Alton had first copied a line of the inscription. Under this line appeared the corresponding line from the Ulonga chant, under that his reconstructed pronunciation, and under that the English equivalent.

After a quick, cursory glance, Graham read the fourth lines consecutively and thus obtained an uninterrupted translation. Wrinkles formed on his forehead as he read:

Awaken! Far titans of time and of space and of being, creators of life, creators of death, creators of energy. On the appointed day set by the stars fall through the stars from your great world beyond to this little world you have created. Claim your own and return to your great world beyond. Oh Keeper of the Seal, take from us that which the titans have given and that which is theirs, even as they shall take on the appointed day set by the stars. We are yours as we are theirs. Awaiting them, we summon you. Far titans, awaken!

.Far titans? What far titans? Who was the "Keeper of the Seal?" Could that be the fantastic little figurine? And what was the "great world beyond"? Was the ritual anything more than a senseless jumble?

Graham sighed wearily. Alton had translated the inscription down to the middle geometric designs of the green seal, but he had not carried them through the lower half of the symbols. He had only progressed as far as setting down the pronunciation of the final half, so that Graham could at least speak the symbols, if he were sufficiently foolhardy. There stood the rest of the symbols, unsolved, perhaps unsolvable, challenging him with their enigmatic whorls and spirals.

IX

THE HAUNTED

TIIE lines on Graham's face were bleaker and he looked almost gaunt when he had finished reading Alton's letter. Whatever he did brought a train of disaster. Every attempt at fathoming the mystery led him into deeper entanglements and fresh morasses. He had asked for assistance from two colleagues. Liska had suffered an eerie death, while Alton had apparently become a victim, though indirectly, of the same overwhelming manifestation that Graham had experienced on the wrecked train.

For a long time, he stared moodily through the window. A fiery sun was setting in a coppery sky. The roofs of buildings and the tops of trees glowed with a dull flame. Murky shadows lengthened on the ground. It had been a sweltering day. The sky was like a furnace. The sun burned with the glare of a bloodshot eye, and the buildings wavered through heat-waves. The myriad noise of a metropolis drifted up, and the ants of the city crawled their way. He hardly noticed them, for he looked far away, beyond the city, and beyond the world.

The newspapers lay on the table behind him, but he could not forget the sudden epidemic of odd events that had happened all over the globe. What blight was this that had come upon the world, a blight that flourished wherever men were to be found?

Wearily he turned his gaze from the flame-tipped buildings and crimson horizon to the articles he had clipped
from the recent dailies. He examined them again, weighing
the implications of the theme that was common to them
all.

A dispatch from Cape Town announced:

NATIVE UNREST SPREADS

The outbreak of violence among tribes of the interior is
spreading rapidly. First reported last week from Rhodesia and
the Transvaal, the uprisings have now extended to Tanganyika, the Congo, and other areas as far north as the Sudan.

Authorities have as yet taken no repressive measures. It is
felt in official circles that the natives are participating in tribal
ceremonies of ritual importance. However, it is understood
that troops are available in case counter-action becomes necessary.

There is some doubt as to the exact cause and nature of
the unrest which has made the drums beat incessantly day and
night throughout all Africa.

Lt. Col. James Mulreavy, returning from Tanganyika, states
that the natives there are at the wildest pitch of excitement he
has ever seen. He believes that the witch doctors are responsible. Every sort of black magic is being practised. Human
sacrifices, he declares, have been made in large numbers. Flagel-
lation, torture, and primitive rites of a degrading nature are
common. He adds that the witch doctors claim they are preparing for the return of their gods.

According to another observer, Mr. T. H. Wilson-Grant,
a licensed trader at Mepli, the tribes have developed a kind
of group madness. He says that weird images and objects have
suddenly appeared in great quantity, that the natives are in a

dangerous state of revolt, and that the witchmen are using fear and superstition to inflame the tribes. He reports also that they are proclaiming the visitation of some monstrous deity from the skies.

Another story came from Calcutta:

PRANJHIPOK QUIET
UNDER MARTIAL LAW

The rioting that swept Pranjhipok last night has been brought under control by national police. More than two thousand Moslems, Hindus, Sikhs, and foreigners were killed during the outburst of violence that came shortly after sunset.

Armed with knives, daggers, pistols, and rifles, the population suddenly ran amok, attacking each other as well as occupants of the European quarter. In addition to the known dead, several thousand were injured. Serious fires are still burning in many parts of the city but have begun to subside. Widespread looting that accompanied the violence ended with the imposition of martial law. Property damage is estimated in the millions.

The reason for the rioting has not yet been established, but religious mania is believed responsible. Shrines, temples, and holy men were literally besieged by mobs. There is some obscure rumor current to the effect that ancient gods are about to be reincarnated.

The Moslems claim that Mohammed is ready to make his second appearance on earth. The Buddhists, Brahmans, Tsaoists, and members of other sects assert that their respective deities are returning.

Additional troops are en route to Pranjhipok from Calcutta and Bombay.

Of a different kind was a feature that originated in New York:

KALEN TAKES OWN LIFE

Artist Leaps From
Park Avenue Studio

The body of Glen Kalen, internationally famous painter and sculptor, was found yesterday at 4:15 P.M. in the courtyard of the Wilmyn Arms, where he had resided for the last three years.

He left two short notes in his studio. One to a friend identified as Marva said, "Good-bye, dear, join me as soon as you can. I would rather take my own life than be taken by *them*."

The second note was addressed to an unidentified "Septhulchu." It merely said, "When you come, I at least will be gone."

In Kalen's studio were found a number of remarkable paintings which experts say are among his best works, though all are highly fantastic. One of them is strikingly three-dimensional, entirely in shades of green, and depicts a kind of luminous fog or sea through which terrifying shapes are beginning to emerge. A startling piece of sculpture also was discovered. This bore some resemblance to an Easter Island statue, and showed a demonic creature engulfing a mass of tiny human beings.

Kalen's friends reported that his behavior had been very unusual recently, and that he seemed worried, although he had ample means and no known illness or personal problems. According to them, he had become depressed after complaining of being disturbed by remarkable dreams. These nightmares persisted so vividly that he attempted to capture them in his work. He made references to a great calamity that he asserted would overwhelm mankind.

While no witnesses have been found, police are convinced that in a fit of despondency or temporary insanity he leaped from his studio window on the eighth floor.

The next addition to the batch of clippings originated in San Francisco:

SLAYER KILLS 9TH VICTIM

The body of Jane Dorel was discovered early this morning in Oakland Bay, the ninth victim of the maniac who has spread a reign of terror in the San Francisco area. Three children, two men, and four women have been murdered in the past ten days.

An autopsy disclosed that the 19-year-old blond had been dead at least forty-eight hours. Like the other victims of the slayer, she had been murdered and the body then mutilated. The murderer made more than one hundred gouges before pushing the body into the Bay.

Police are without clues to the slayer, and have not yet located the actual site of the killings and mutilations.

"The murders are completely senseless," according to Police Chief Heggens. "None of the victims was tortured, and none of the women attacked or raped. The only thing that the killings have in common is that each victim was strangled with piano wire and that the bodies were then gouged or pitted in the same gruesome manner. Obviously they are the work of a homicidal maniac."

A curious item from an obituary page related to the death of Aubrey Lellith, a young poet who had died by his own hand, leaving behind him no explanation for his act, except a fragment of a poem which he had left unfinished.

The fragment in its entirety consisted of only a half-dozen lines:

The titans will waken on valley and highland,
 When four-dimensioned vaults dissolve and open wide;
They will spew from the void and advance from Easter Island,
 From time-gulfs and planes of space they will glide.

The titans have prophecied the day of returning
 When the stars have attained the positions they proclaimed
And skies turn to flame

Another news feature concerned a catastrophe in Bavaria:

A general alarm has been broadcast throughout Bavaria warning the inhabitants that more than twenty of the insane who escaped yesterday are still at liberty.

A full account of the disaster has now been pieced together, after thorough investigation by Dr. Hugo Bräuning, superintendent of the Heussen State Hospital for Criminal Insane. At sundown a spontaneous uproar swept the whole asylum where approximately three hundred dangerously insane inmates were confined. They screamed of impending doom and wingy things coming down from above.

Reserve guards were immediately ordered on duty, but attempts to quiet the inmates failed. Five men in the left wing rushed two guards who opened fire, killing three of the maniacs. The remaining two overpowered and fatally injured both guards.

During the assault the rear wing had been set afire. The fire spread beyond control while other guards were herding the inmates to the recreation area. A general riot ensued.

Thirty-eight inmates died in the holocaust, seventy-one were injured, five guards were killed and nine others wounded. About thirty-five inmates escaped, of whom only a dozen have been recaptured.

On the walls of the charred cells the search parties found remains of many weird drawings that had an unusual similarity. These portrayed monsters crushing or sweeping away or digesting human figures. Dr. Bräuning states that an identical obsession, a mass madness, appears to have seized the inmates.

Graham had numerous other clippings, with the same thread running through them all. They possessed a common element in that they concerned an impending visitation from a great world to a little world, from superior beings to microscopic men. What did they mean? Was it mere coincidence that these events were occurring all over the world? Everywhere, allusions to titanic forces, equivocal gods that returned from beyond or outside. A blight seemed to be creeping into man, a disease the more deadly because its nature was unknown, its origin unknown, its purpose unknown.

The clipping on top of the pile lingered longest in his thoughts. He had read it first and last. It concerned an airline pilot in Santiago:

Chilean officials are preparing to send an expedition to Easter Island, on the basis of statements made yesterday by pilot Juan Cortil of Chilean National Airways. The aviator, on a test flight for the proposed service to Australia, reported that violent radio disturbances are active around Easter Island, and of increasing intensity. Near the center of the island he saw a greenish haze. While flying over this area, his plane became severely damaged, as though it had struck a solid object. Cortil managed to fly about three hundred miles toward Chile before he sighted a freighter with which he had established radio contact, and crashed into the ocean.

Cortil asserts that he saw no signs of volcanic activity at Easter Island. He claims that he flew his plane at an altitude of no more than one hundred feet while investigating the greenish haze. The haze, he insisted, surrounded a peculiar small green statue that stood in one of the old craters. Because his attention was fastened on this object he failed to see the large bird which he believes struck the plane and caused the damage.

Cortil could offer no explanation for the phenomena which he claimed to have seen.

The following morning, Graham took his seat on the Transatlantic stratoliner, for the first leg of his long flight. He passed the time studying various notes and data, and bringing his old diary up to date.

X

GRAHAM'S DIARY

THE dark side of the moon or the outer nebulae may contain mysteries deeper and more puzzling than any which I have met on earth; and in the abysses outside the known universe it is not impossible that stranger enigmas than I have found may await whatever traveler spans first the immensity between. These things may be, yet they seem of small importance compared with that daily riddle which has accompanied man during the whole span of his existence, and to which no solution has yet been found. Let the astronomer scrutinize the most distant star and speculate about its origin and composition. I scrutinize the nearest man, and speculate about his origin and composition which present the greatest riddle of all. There have been many attempts at explanation, but the truth eludes us all; and the atheist is one with the mystic in splendid failure.

Let me begin at the origin of all things for me, and try to bring at least an apparently orderly development to the meaningless chaos that is life. Of my parents I know little for they died during my childhood, leaving me, their only child, a moderate income under the care of a guardian. I chiefly remember my father as something of an impractical dreamer, and my mother as a woman of uncanny intuition verging on mysticism. I can not imagine how I inherited from them the inquiring mind that is my single good attribute.

The death of my parents made me feel absolutely alone in the world at an early age. And the change in my surroundings merely drove me into further reticence and reliance on my own resources. It also started me to wondering about the purpose of life and death. My personal sense of loss did not, however, make me a recluse or lead me into the morbid psychology of self-pity as it might easily have done. Instead, I developed an active and expanding curiosity about the whole meaning or cause of man's existence, his short life and death as an individual, his long life and death in races and species.

I remained, however, solitary in nature and had no wish for intimate companions or friends. I never cared for group pastimes at the schools I attended, had no interest in sports, and virtually none in social affairs. I was deeply absorbed in my studies, and tended to regard people in much the same way as I regarded insects or bacteria under a microscope, as subjects for observation and analysis.

By the time I entered Oxford, I had pursued a number of different fields of interest quite extensively, but only for short intervals. I had a lucky faculty of absorbing what I read as rapidly as I could turn the pages of books. I had delved into philosophy rather broadly, from Plato and Lucretius to Spengler and Americus. I studied the great religions of the world, comparing their tenets and creeds. I examined their rich cousins, witchcraft and sorcery, spiritualism and black magic. From these diversions of the mind, I advanced to fields of more precise knowledge, and spent months at a time in concentration upon one science after another—geology, astronomy, chemistry, biology, psychology. The more I read the less I knew, and the greater my information the smaller my understanding about the mystery of life in general, mankind in particular.

Was there, indeed, a single thing which I did know and did understand completely? The ripple of wind in trees outside my window, the growth of leaves in spring, the color of a pearl, waves on a beach, the sidewalks of a city street, buying a woman for a night, the grain of sand I stepped on, all held as much and as little meaning as the sky above me. I felt, curiously enough, rather like a detective; I was always on the trail of a fugitive whom I never caught; examining clues in an effort to discover an agent whom I never identified. I invariably came to blind ends. The problem trailed off into obscurity, vanished before the dawn of history and in the mist of unrecorded beginnings.

I do not know where my researches might have led me if an event had not occurred which changed the course of my life and sent me off on a different path.

I fell in love, very deeply, and probably with all the more intensity because of my previous indifference to women, and my limited experience with them. There was, however, a provision in my inheritance depriving me of both the income and the principal if I married before my twenty-first birthday. It would take almost another year to obey that restriction, but neither Iris nor I could wait. I am glad that we did not. We accepted the natural solution and took a little flat. We would live together and become married the day after I reached majority. It was then the end of the school term, and instead of spending the summer touring Europe as I had planned, I spent it with Iris.

She was a couple of years older than I, and much more experienced. She knew the art of love as completely, I suppose, as any woman could, and in her early role of teacher she found me an ardent pupil, and if not as talented as she, at least fully co-operative and with insatiable enthusiasm. She was a blond with hair the hue of butternut wood. I would not have called her face beautiful when I first met her, through her mouth was full and sensuous; her nose was pert and short, her chin somewhat narrow, but she had lovely blue eyes and a wonderfully firm, exciting body. I came, in time, to regard her with that special devotion that transforms the beloved into perfect beauty. The days were as breathless as the nights were a constant rapture. I had not dreamed it possible to experience such overwhelming physical ecstasy and such rare happiness of mind.

For Iris proved remarkably stimulating company. She had a running laughter that found delight in little things that would annoy the average persons. She had studied and practised dancing as an art, a profession, which gave her a special grace and rhythm of motion. She possessed a mind both agile and open, with a broad range of interests and an expert knowledge of ballet, theatrical costuming, music, and poetry. I never tired of conversation with her; indeed, conversation, like love, became an exhilarating game which we continually perfected through experimental variations.

When Iris became pregnant, she blossomed anew with a luminous and magnetic radiance that made her an exquisite joy to behold. I loved her more deeply than ever, and found an ampler richness in being with her, a more fruitful abundance. Life with her had become a pure exaltation.

One day in August I went to see my guardian in connection with my inheritance and approaching majority. Upon my return, I walked gaily into our little flat, and the happiness poured away from me in a black ebb-tide, never to return.

Iris had been murdered. She lay on the floor, her face slashed and a stab-wound in her heart. Eventually, Scotland Yard caught the murderer, a jealous ballet-dancer and former lover of hers, who had brooded over her life with me. He had intended to kill us both. He went to the gallows.

For months I walked in a daze of hopeless despair. I crossed busy streets indifferent to traffic. Not a vehicle ever harmed me. Once I swam six miles into the Atlantic, intending simply to keep on swimming westward. A sailing yawl overtook me and hauled me aboard. One night after hours of bleak and grief-laden tossing, I swallowed an entire bottle of sleeping-tablets. Fire broke out in the building, the fire-fighters discovered me and rushed me to a hospital. It seemed as though a wilfully perverse fate, having robbed me of my happiness, was determined that I live for ever to endure the memory of tragedy a thousand times over and over.

I could not pursue any studies that year. Often I felt that

something in me must break, that the burden had become unbearable, that the mind must shatter. But it would not. Each morning there was the clear light of day, and the ruthless persistence of the world, in its hard and relentless reality. I did not want it, but there it was.

Since I could not study and had no interest in anything around me, and since my absolute indifference to life only resulted in prolonging my life, I finally determined to travel. Perhaps a fatal accident would occur in other surroundings. I could not hope to forget Iris, not though I lived for a hundred years or a million years, or took the nights to a thousand other women.

Iris had once said that she wanted to visit Egypt, some day. I bought passage to Egypt.

During the journey, I found myself preoccupied with the old riddle under the impact of recent grief. The lives of those closest to me had ended—father, mother, lover. The bitterness in my heart and the turning screw of anguish made me wonder what grotesque source or cause or power ever produced anything so senseless as human life. The poignant regrets of my individual life were nothing compared to the huge despairs of races and nations through eras of time.

I tried to merge my unhappiness with that of other individuals, with that of all humanity. The attempt did not partly succeed, then, or wholly succeed, ever. For brief periods I even came to hate the memory of Iris for having cast so powerful a spell over me. But always my emotions burned themselves out into the black cinder of despair.

Then, one morning, I found myself gazing at the Sphinx. It fascinated me as greatly as it had captured the imaginations of other men. I spent hours with it.

That great, enigmatic structure drew me across a gulf of centuries. I was enthralled and quickened by its inhuman stoniness. I puzzled on its meaning and origin and purpose. The lure of ancient ruins had fallen upon me.

Here was a way to compensate for current unhappiness, by research into relics of the remote past, by exploring the remains of antiquity. I recognized it, at the outset, as a form of escape mechanism. But archaeology was the special field in which my life could find a measure of expression during its remaining years.

I studied the pyramids. I went into Tibet and Mongolia. I examined the stone circles scattered in various parts of England, and investigated Stonehenge. I penetrated the jungles of Yucatan and scrutinized the remnants of Mayan civilization. I ransacked forgotten literatures for their references to Atlantis and Lemuria. Angkor-Wat rang to my footsteps. Many and many an hour I spent at that fabulous and unique marvel, the great golden Dial of Nyamba.

But more than any of these, Easter Island haunted my mind. I lived for months upon the island, studying its colossal stone platforms and enormous statues.

Each of these sites and a dozen others that I examined offered questions I could not answer. Why did their builders employ so largely the circle and the pyramid? Easter Island alone was ringed in concentric circles with its inexplicable remains. And whence came a certain singular uniformity in the conception of the builders? Above all, whence came this giantism which was everywhere apparent, this striving to suggest or embody vast size? What series of cataclysms or holocausts had utterly wiped out so many of the races that had built them?

There were periods when my interest ebbed away, when the old despair returned and I brooded about Iris, when I lay under the grip of such profound melancholy that nothing seemed worth while. These periods would last for weeks or months, and I would slowly emerge from them only by departing on new explorations.

During one of these travels, to Paru-Sai in the heart of Tibet, on a great mountain facing southeastward, I encountered a solitary shrine with a shrivelled old Sekhite, priest of a vanishing cult, and obtained shelter for the night. He spoke a precise, scholarly kind of English. He was one of the wisest and most learned men I ever knew. We talked for most of the night. I told him of my journeys, my explorations, the purpose underlying my inquiries. I mentioned my curiosity about the origin of many remains, about their vast size, and about my speculations concerning that ultimate riddle, the origins of man.

He listened with inscrutable repose on his dark and wizened face. When I had finished he took his frail old body to somer inner recess, and emerged bearing a book whose ivory covers bore strange symbols inlaid in gold. He opened it to show a score of parchment leaves. Their age was incomputable, their language unknown to me. And obviously more remote from Sanskrit than Sanskrit is from

English. He read me a passage from that record out of anterior time:

When the stars are come to the positions prophesied and fixed in the pattern prescribed, then will the titans awaken and return. Earth shall open. Out of crypts deeper than the clouds are high shall the Keeper of the Seal issue forth a summons to the titans. The Keeper of the Seal shall become even as the titans and take his place on Crltul Thr. The waters shall boil, the earth shall split, the lightnings break and the skies burn. From their plane outside the stars shall the titans descend. All life shall be claimed by them who fashioned us from the dust that quickened and the fire that consumed. These things shall come to pass when the titans awaken when the stars are set, lest there come he who challenges the Keeper of the Seal with the secret of secrets. If he challenge the Keeper, and if he succeed, then shall the Keeper return unto stone and the titans wait until the great sphere of stars shall reach again the position predetermined. And the Keeper of the Seal shall remain on the axis from Crltul Thr to Mrcg.

I made a memorandum of this cryptic ritual, at that time meaningless to me.

My host then turned to the last pages of the antique volume, which consisted of maps. The first map showed the stars as no living man had ever seen them, as they might have looked a million years or more in the past. The second map showed them as they would be a couple of decades in the future—the Sekhite named the year, for his knowledge of astronomy was prodigious. The final map interested me most of all, for it showed a recognizable outline of the earth and its continents.

The land masses and the seas, however, were radically different from the existing surface of earth. My memory of geology proved helpful, for I recalled hypothetical maps of earth's surface as it had appeared during various periods of geologic time; and the map before me corresponded to the end of the Miocene Age or the opening of the Pliocene. Thus it represented conditions on a time-scale approximating 1,500,000 years ago.

This map, furthermore, had one striking characteristic, which was a line or axis running from what is now Easter Island to what is now the vicinity of Stonehenge. I asked my host what the line signified, but he merely pointed to the ritual words I had written down. Who or what was the Keeper of the Seal? And did his "axis from Crltul Thr to Mrcg" refer to the line from Easter Island to Stonehenge? I asked, but received no answers.

For several years thereafter, I continued my investigations through near and far areas of the world. I made the oldest remains of antiquity, the most primitive monuments of man, my special study.

The words of the Sekhite echoed across the years, and I made several field trips to the Stonehenge district, but without any noteworthy discoveries.

Eventually I accepted a position which led to my becoming curator of the Ludbury Museum.

I continued my wide reading. I acquainted myself with the electrogenetic theory of life, the theory that what we call life exists only while a positive-negative interchange of electrical impulses occurs in the body. I familiarized myself with the new mathematics, the Einstein theories, four-dimensional geometry. I sifted the various hypotheses about the origin of the world—the theologic, the nebular, the planetary, and so on. I pursued an extensive study of myths, legends, and folklore of all races.

My inquiries and analyses led me to a choice between two mutually exclusive conclusions, only one of which could be true. Either human life originated in some spontaneous fashion upon earth; or it was brought to earth from elsewhere. If it originated on earth, I probably would never know how or why; but if it was brought from outside, another alternative arose: either it came accidentally, on a meteorite or on a drift of spores or germs or primary seed; or it came as the result of deliberate intention, of willful intelligence and purpose. If it came accidentally again I would probably never know why or how; but if it came as the result of a purposing will or rational intelligence, then there might be hope of progress.

Thus my general line of thought developed, and my explorations continued during periodic leaves of absence from the Ludbury Museum.

But nothing in recent years gave me such a great stimulus as the fateful day when I read an account of a weird green image discovered at Isling. The reference to it strongly suggested that the sculpture might be the Keeper of the Seal referred to by the prehistoric volume in the shrine at Paru-Sai; and so extraordinary were the implications that I immediately went to Isling. I not only found that cosmic object, I discovered a bottomless well that plunged deep beneath earth; and I nearly lost my life on my return, for when I ran my fingers across a series of bizarre symbols carved in the base of the image, monstrous and terrifying phenomena occurred, in the vast voice and the fantastic vision.

There could only be two possible explanations of that eldritch adventure. Either I was the victim of constant hallucinations, or forces and powers beyond any with which I was familiar had manifested themselves.

I proceeded on the basis that this latter assumption was correct. In that case, my fingering of the queer and cryptic signs carved in the idol's base had been the immediate cause producing the phenomena I observed.

What was the nature of the mechanism? I had apparently issued a signal or sent out a warning. I could find no adequate explanation in terms of wave-theories, or in velocities of the order of light-rays. It was, rather, as though the statuette somehow transmitted, at multiplied and stepped-up intensity, my thoughts about it, and brought a quick reaction from the receiver somewhere in other-time and other-space.

What solution there was lay in the statuette itself. Since it bore no resemblance to any element or mineral or rock of earth, it could only be of non-terrestrial origin, and as such not subject to the laws of earth; indeed, it must re-

spond to laws that were totally alien to those governing
matter and energy as we know them. If this were true, the
image must have been brought to the world, planted, as
it were, by beings from elsewhere, for some definite reason;
a specific purpose of such importance that any tampering
with it immediately called forth some sort of guardian.
Furthermore, the very nature of the statuette, its outstanding artistry, denoted craftsmanship relative to a civilization of the very highest degree.

The vision that I saw, I reasoned, must be either a
guardian, raised by some unfamiliar means of communication of a kind unknown to our scientists, or perhaps the
entity itself which had at some period in the past placed
the sculpture near Isling. Why had it done so? When had
the teleportation been accomplished? For what purpose?
And who or what was the nature of that entity?

Why had the mysterious protecting slab or seal been
placed over the vertical well at Isling? Whence came the
mammoth heap of bones? They may have been sacrifices,
I thought, made over an extended continuum of time to
some deity, for they comprised modern man and his prede-
cessors back to earlier human remains than any that had
ever been previously discovered. The sacrificial cult theory
seemed possible; but more likely, that the bones were those
of victims who at various times had stumbled on and
tinkered with the time-trap. Trapped for what purpose—
for the flesh and the life to be consumed, as it were, dissolved and transmitted elsewhere, perhaps for sustenance,
perhaps for study? Could that strange material of the green

figurine be organic in a different universe? Or if not organic, at least a kind of force or existence comparable to what we call life? I felt that I was piecing together the clues in my long detective pursuit through time and space, that the ambiguities were beginning to assume a clear form.

I devoted considerable reflection to my escape from the subterranean corridor, my exit into Stonehenge, and the remarkable properties of the slab or seal protecting the well. In all these there was definite indication of ultra-Euclidean geometry; of the operation of laws of a universe or existence differing from ours.

Stonehenge itself might be a prehistoric structure erected from superstition, or from knowledge of the great corridor lying underneath. It might even be that the possessors of these innumerous bones, when the clothing of mortality still enveloped them in far off gulfs of time forgotten, had deliberately entered the subterranean necropolis by way of the four-dimensional seal, not by accident but by compulsion, and their flesh, their intelligence, their life-identity dissolved and transmitted by unknown force to a dimension of time-space-life remote from us, yet possibly quite near at hand under the laws of that hyper-universe, that hyper-space, that hyper-time.

I examined in detail the photographs which I had taken of the markings on the greenish portal to the vertical well. I was especially interested in the two sets of astronomical charts. I easily recognized them as identical with the maps in the Sekhite's ancient manuscript. There must have been a purpose, deliberate, exact, prophetic, behind the two

sets. I remembered, also, the other curious map in the
manuscript, a chart of earth's surface as it looked a million
and a half years ago. Then, too, I had among my notes a
copy of the passage which the aged Sekhite had read to me.

A pattern began to emerge from these isolated pieces. I
made an effort at reconstructing events of the very distant
past. I tried to adopt a new and wholly alien viewpoint; not
the viewpoint of a man upon earth to whom the universe
around him was something gigantic beyond understanding;
but the viewpoint of a total outsider, an inhabitant of a
super-cosmos, to whom this universe was something in-
finitesimal, a mere speck, a mere drop on a slide under a
microscope. I conceived of that entity or group of entities,
in their super-cosmos outside ours, as experimenting, plant-
ing what was to them a tiny germ, an invisible virus of
human life on the culture under the slide; and leaving a
device to record the growth of that virus, to imprison units
of it in a sort of test-tube, the time-trap. I thought of them
as having established a cycle, a cycle of 1,500,000 years on
our time-scale, but a cycle that might be only 1,500,000
seconds on their time-scale, or the equivalent of a little less
than three weeks.

And if the first map indicated the period when the titans
from outside had first come to earth or implanted the virus
of human life, then the second map must indicate when
that experiment would be completed. In that case, whatever happened, whatever phenomena occurred, would
take place at one end of the Easter Island-Stonehenge axis,
and take place very soon.

The more I reflected, the more I conceived the outside

entities as the originators of the human virus on earth. For what purpose? Perhaps merely as a culture-medium, to develop a specially virulent strain for combatting some deadly disease in their super-existence. And at the end of three weeks in their hyper-time, the end of one and one-half million years in our time, they are returning, perhaps to collect the result of their experiment, perhaps to destroy it and begin another.

One million five hundred thousand years? Why not? The whole universe as we know it may be but a complex molecule or cell in the lowliest part of their super-universe, just as a molecule or cell to us may be part of a tobacco plant, of tobacco mosaic disease.

And the full one and one-half million years of murder and love and hatred and death and birth and invention and slow progress toward civilization might be only days in the time-scale of those entities exterior to our universe. A little fly that we know, the ephemeris, lives it full life in a day, and is gone. But to the ephemeris itself, that day must seem as long as man's life of a hundred years does to him. So, to the beings of the greater universe of which ours is only the tiniest particle, our concept of one and one-half million years may be but a few passing days or weeks.

And the strange green image was the guide to the experiment of life, the Keeper of the Seal. It is as if the chemists, those enigmatic inhabitants of a super-universe above time and beyond space, to which our universe compares only as a mote does to the solar system, had inoculated a fluid drop underneath a microscope in an ultra-cosmic laboratory; an experiment that resulted in a germ multiplying to millions upon millions of germs or viruses during the incubation period of two or three weeks; and now that the human virus has flourished, the experiment is to be completed. By oblivion? By transmutation? By variation?

I do not know. But all this eerie play of forces will reach its climax, I believe, on Easter Island, among the burial blocks and the lordly statues that strew the island. For the stars are come to the position prescribed in the chart on the green slab at Isling and the map in the Sekhite's manuscript.

What shall I do if the beings from a greater universe manifest themselves? What can I do? How can I challenge them? Obviously, nothing as low as humanity or the forces prevailing on earth can affect them, for they would be responsive only to laws of an exterior universe, a space and time outside of ours, a higher complexity, an alien structure of life, a superior order of power and energy.

I would need to meet them on their own level. But how? Is there a key or clue among all the notes I have made?

And what though I face the titans and challenge them? Can I discover the nature of their universe? How they originated and what the characteristics of their civilization are? If these entities account for human life, what created them or brought them into existence? A still more immense universe in a still more unfathomable plane of multi-dimensional scope, with dimmer and more recessive reasons for realms and states of duration completely beyond any hope of comprehension?

Are the titans organic in nature? Or inorganic, some

doubtful anomaly of compounds imbued with thinking energy? Or some substance of which we know nothing, some ulterior product of ulterior universes, partaking of matter that is outside our grasp? May they not be wholly insubstantial? Pure energy, pure concept, pure force, intangible, beyond analysis, without definite or constant form or resolvable constituents? If a gas could talk, or lightning deliberate, or mercury breathe, I would understand the titans better.

I have no answers. I can only wait and watch to see what, if anything, emerges from the web of Easter Island.

XI

EASTER ISLAND

THE feeling that he was alone on Easter Island came as a surprise to Graham. In the past there had always been natives, and usually a few representatives of the Chilean government.

The plane he had chartered had left him with enough supplies for a month, though he had ordered it to return in a week.

The silence of the island was extraordinary; he heard the everlasting wash of the sea, and the dull roar of breakers, but aside from those sounds and the whispering wind, nothing.

He had reached the island in late afternoon, too late for exploration. He cooked a light supper on a portable gasoline burner, and watched the sun slide down. A sprinkling of stars shone feebly; the damp atmosphere made visibility poor. He saw no trace of fires anywhere, nor heard the sound of a single voice. Inquisitive natives usually were waiting for any arrival, so rare were visitors to the island. He missed their presence.

Graham passed a solitary night, troubled with dreams.

When morning came, he began a systematic exploration of the island. He remembered its topography clearly from his previous stay upon it. Rano-Raraku—there was no mistaking the volcanic king of the island. He got his bearings from it and set out.

By noon he had verified the truth of his first impression. There was not a single other human being on Easter Island. What had happened? Had the natives died off since his earlier visit fifteen years ago? Had the government agents removed them to Chile? Or could some great fear have driven them away? Had disease wiped them out? Had they migrated of their own volition? There had once been a report that the island had temporarily sunk; a ship, driven far off its course in a wild January gale, sighted no land where Easter Island should have been. Had the island been engulfed, then spewed forth again by the boiling waters from some upheaval on the ocean floor? Graham conceded its possibility, though patches of grass grew in shallow spaces, and a few dwarfed pandanus and coconut trees fought for a starved existence.

He had never seen so desolate an island. The absence of its former inhabitants had eliminated all trace of anything friendly or familiar. It was the barrenest land on all the seas, volcanic, basaltic, black, with porous, infertile soil. Jagged rocks lined its shores, boulders lay thick everywhere, sharp masses sprawled by cliffs that rose precipitous. And from Akahanga along the shore to Toatoa enormous fallen statutes loomed irregularly, giants bowled over, while in the sculptors' workshop on the slopes of Rano Raraku far away, hewn and half-hewn colossi looked stonily out to sea. And the eternal ocean beat a solemn requiem on the rocks, a swelling and falling dirge incessantly, day

and night, through irrecoverable years, a perpetual chant
to the monsters carved by forgotten hands.

   Inhuman giants! Immutable mockery of imperious faces
that even the ravaging storms and winds could only erode,
never erase! Who had gouged these titanic blocks of the
memorial funeral platforms from the cliffs? What vanished
race had left a heritage of thousands of vast, forbidding
sculptures that watched the sea as if waiting—waiting for
what? Over all Easter Island had hung an atmosphere of
mystery ever since the Dutch navigator Roggewein chanced
upon it early in the eighteenth century. Every man who
had ever visited that lonely spot in the turbulent south
seas of the mid-Pacific felt the pull of its unfathomed
riddle, a riddle that Graham considered more baffling than
the Sphinx. An army of men working for generations
could hardly have accomplished the feat of hewing and
erecting these thousands upon thousands of carved basalt
and conglomerate statues and memorial cairns or funeral
platforms. Surely the island could never have supported
more than a fraction of the hords of workers whose labor
would have been required with the primitive tools then
available. Or had something more than human hands and
human energy helped in the shaping of those great ones
and their placement in position? For that matter, why had
the rings of burial piles been raised and the megalithic
statues set up? And why had all this tremendous task been
abruptly deserted at its very peak of accomplishment so
that unfinished giants and roughly cut monoliths sprawled
where they had been when work stopped? Half a dozen

scientific expeditions had gone to the island at various times, but never a one returned with anything more than guesswork and conjecture at the identity of the sculptors, during what century they had toiled, and for what inscrutable purpose.

And now Graham felt something even more forbidding in the aspect of Easter Island, for always before, the handful of human beings upon it had softened the mental impact of the haughty colossi; but now there was no one else, not a voice or a footfall to be heard, and the manner of their disappearance added one more puzzle to the records of the island. The wind blew gustily, had been blowing stiffly since noon; whitecaps rose and broke and rose again, and the long, surging waves crashed with massive booming upon the jagged beach-cliffs and boulder masses. A strange, shuddering disturbance gave an alien unrest to the air. Upon Graham descended the apprehension that man feels in the presence of an unknown and antagonistic universe.

He spent the entire afternoon exploring the south coast from Akahangi along the beach toward Rano Raraku. Many a minute he stared at the imperturbable monsters that stood proudly, or lay toppled, yet lordly and conquering even in their fall. The thin curve of lips, the strong nose, the brooding eyes and high cheek-bones were the sculptured record of a race of masters. The sun began to sink, and shadows crept along the ground, every hollow held a handful of dusk, a deeper frown seemed to settle upon the faces of the stilled colossi, and ever the wind whispered eerily and the sea thunderously chanted its eternal dirge. Then it was that Graham rounded a great boulder near Toatoa, and there in the rubble before him saw a deep, recently made rut extending to the shore. With a feeling of supernatural yet acutely realistic awareness, he observed the unaccountable way in which that deep rut suddenly ended; yet not wholly unaccountable, for the print of a gigantic tread fissured the iron-hard ground, and a hundred yards inland sank another huge impression that had sheared off and pulverized tons of basalt from one of the largest burial platforms, and like a tremendous warning those tremendous pits progressed toward Rano Raraku rising sinister in the distance and darkness of twilight.

Something had slid ashore out of the seas, and something else had met it and borne it to the workshop of the gods on Rano Raraku. Graham gave a long, appraising glance at that bleak and volcanic cone; then he turned and went back to his camp.

The wind prowled curiously; shadows gathered fast, and his imagination created a dream-shape out of each boulder and every sculpture; but was it imagination that from infinite distance rolled the echos of cosmic stirrings, neither of laughter nor contempt, but only of supreme indifference? The wind was blowing stronger and stronger, a rock mass fell, and the sea crashed harshly against cliffs that crumbled. He sent a quick look backwards toward Rano Raraku, then turned no more. For he thought he had seen a wild, phantasmal light flowing and glowing and gathering mistily over the peak of Rano Raraku, a light the more terrifying because it was like no color he had ever before seen. He could not describe it. He could not face it. He could not accept it. He could not relate it to any previous experience. Hideous, ambiguous, fluid, exultant, viable, it carried a terrifying implication of some unimaginable life, some visible intelligence independent of body, concentrating and yet on the verge of expansion. It flickered and pulsed over the center of the cone, yet seemed to extend limitlessly into space and beyond space. But of this, or any part of this, he could not be completely sure, for after that one instant of frozen stupefaction, he turned and continued his way back. The wind whooped dismally, the restless sea boiled against the bases of black rock masses, and the stony statues stood sentient with grave and ominous prophecy as he passed them.

He prepared a quick supper, but when he had finished he could not remember the taste of it. His actions had been mechanical, for the phenomena preoccupied his mind. By lamplight he examined many of his notes, and in the dark hours he did a strange thing, moving his lips silently, as though rehearsing a speech, yet careful to make no sound. It was very late when he retired, later still before he slept; since, throughout the evening and night, the impact of forces generating over Easter Island increased perceptibly in power and strength. While Graham felt a tangible weight, a pressure that increased hourly, miles away from him a flowing, unearthly, searching color played around Rano Raraku and shot toward the remote abysses of space, inquiring, shifting, listening, waiting, answering, and expanding.

Graham finally dozed off into fitful sleep, a sleep broken by nervous awakenings; and always he heard the rising skirl of winds, and the heavy pounding of the sea; and once he sensed the echo of far voices, mirthless, inhuman, as stony as the primal rocks; and once he heard the decrescendo of a cry, but it was his own voice breaking out in the throes of torturing dream. Overhead the vague stars shone hazily, with an unwonted dimness and preternatural weakness, like candles burning low before they flickered quietly out. The loneliness of sea and land and sky was such as he had not believed possible; a complete and unrelieved isolation in which all the world had passed away and he alone remained.

The wind rustled in the pandanus trees and swished the short grasses; it moaned around the rocks and rose shrilly by the cliffs; out at sea it blew in great sweeping gusts like the open-stops of an organ in abysmal spaces; and the Pacific thundered its eternal answer.

So, at last, Graham fell asleep again, and dreamed a dream. He was falling like a comet through gulfs beyond the solar system, but falling faster than any comet, faster than light itself; hurtling onward at such velocity that stars and then galaxies streamed by him like mere fireflies at night, becoming extinguished behind him. Vastness of astronomical distance sped past him and shrank. Then followed a curious distortion: the stars appeared to diminish toward him from ahead and expand away from him behind, until, gradually, he felt that space had become bent in some abstract manner, curved in a dual way, and curved in a many-dimensioned continuum; and the millions upon millions of light-years he had traveled collapsed to the briefest of inter-related arcs; and he was sliding along planes of space, exteriors of time, in an apocryphal emergence.

Then suddenly the galaxies and nebulae lay behind him. They were no more. All the universe had dwindled and vanished in a mote. He had no existence. He drifted through a mid-region beyond all speculation, outside of concept, above theory. After formless chaos, his dream-self came to rest, upon some material substance; and his dream-self was caught in a smear on a slide under observation in a laboratory of many infinities; and beyond it stretched a universe, a measured, simple, elementary, six-dimensional cosmos, the mere molecule of a larger universe beyond it and outside it. And all the universe it had left, Graham's dream-self realized, was lost in the atom on which it now stood, having emerged through the shell; the millions of light-years with all their galaxies now reduced to an invisible speck far down in the structure of that fluid drop which his dream-self occupied.

Where did the progression end? The expanding universes within greater universes? His dream-self half-glimpsed the titans, of a different, more complex, and heightened order of existence, incomprehensible in either the completeness or the detail of their wholly alien, wholly inconceivable aspect, for by no human terms could they be analyzed, they who were outside the range of human senses, outside of time and space. And Graham's dream-self, dwarfed by these other-dimensional titans, trembled; trembled at the hue of living light that never was on sea or land; trembled at the flux of forces and energies and powers that pursued objectives of their own, independent of the titans; trembled at the shifting interchange of pure intelligence and wilful light and active operations of hyper-space and hyper-time; trembled at the soaring citadels of an architecture that adjusted itself automatically to the separate requirements of each inhabitant and each power, so that it simultaneously presented many shapes and occupied many facets of hyper-space and hyper-time; and trembled most of all at the purposes beyond this outside universe, the ultimate goal of the titans which had created the dimensions on which their existence depended and would endure when the foundations and the strange spaces themselves had been consumed.

With the fantastic illogic of dreams, Graham's vision had been compressed into an instant; and all that had passed was merely the tick of a clock in an early and crude scale of time; but now, with the same paradoxical slowness of eternity combined with instantaneous velocity, the titans became aware of him. He saw their fluctuant statures ballooning to other skies and abstruser dimensions, shifting for ever through formless mutations of size and being so that he could never know exactly what they were; imperceptible to mortal senses, perpetually virbrant through cycles of pulsing shape and whirling through immensitudes of superior existence, above apprehension. They knew of his entry, of his presence in their realm, and he knew that they knew; he felt a massive force surge from them, but their thought, their will, their intent, their purpose, expressed in the terms of their alien existence, proved totally incomprehensible to his dream-self; and he found himself receding, diminishing, a rejected interloper, a primordial micro-organism driven back to its proper place among the cells of galaxies and molecules of stars that formed its lowly universe.

Graham awakened with a dry, burning skin, and listened to the dreary swoosh of the rising winds, the somber crash of waters. He slept again.

He dreamed a dream. He walked in dark places, and from afar came faint, ironic laughter; he walked for hours, and sometimes ran, sometimes halted, listening intently; but whether he walked or ran or halted, the cosmic laughter echoed in his ears; nor could he discern any object in the wilderness of gloom; yet he walked on. And the dark places grew darker, and the gusty laughter accompanied him, voiced but voiceless, impersonal and without meaning. And then by his side walked Iris; but he was uncomforted, for the antagonists chuckled mirthlessly as ever before. Side by side they walked, and the darker places grew darkest, and torment assailed him. But there was quiet in Iris; and he became comforted. Had he lost her? It had happened long ago, an old dream that was false. This was now; and Iris walked beside him. Yet hunger deepened; this was now; all else, all past, all gone, only the dream of a dream. In the darkest places his heart called; and the haunting, unforgotten, unforgettable face uplifted, with the clear blue eyes shining into his; and in the ecstasy

of the quiet he bent over and kissed that beloved mouth;
only to press upon naked bone, to peer into empty sockets,
to hold the inmost frame. And distant laughter sounded
in his ears, while from the skiey fastnesses a pillar of weird
radiance pulsed into the heart of Rano Raraku, and deepened hourly in its baleful strength.

In the gray dawn Graham wakened, with the terrors of
darkness and dream exchanged for the fantastic setting of
Easter Island. He arose as exhausted and nervous as if he
had suffered the sleepless vigil of insomnia. Instead of feeling refreshed, he was weary, his mind perplexed with the
equivocal shapes and the prophetic recollections that had
obsessed his inner consciousness. In the mist of morning,
the bulking masses of rocks and stone giants loomed mysterious, impressive, with a threat of superhuman reality.

The wind was still rising, and a steady blow of fine spray
dampened the atmosphere; a spume of foam and shattered
waters broke on the black cliffs, ocean roared farther out,
and the white-caps crashed from higher. As Graham stood
up, a giddiness came over him, as if the island had shaken
beneath his feet. There was a wild and tumultuous note
abroad; the wind whipped his face, and with it came a
foreign element, an uncertain quivering, a restrained turmoil, which he sensed but could not classify. A cirro-
cumulus bank domed the sky far above, but low overhead
a wrack of smoke-dun clouds raced northward, driven by a
forty-mile gale; and in the contrast of the high, serene,
cloud-arch with the lower flying wedges, Graham saw another portent of struggle to come; for the placidness of

cirro-cumulus clouds in the Pacific was a deception of nature, forecasting storms and violent changes of weather, he knew from past experiences.

To the resounding background of sea and wind that beat upon barren Easter Island, Graham started out in early morning and walked along the giants' memorial graveyard. The cyclopean monuments and statues seemed inordinately oppressive; their very presence was a burden that overcast his thoughts. For two days he had not seen a human being, or heard a human voice. His sole company was this profusion of stony monsters and huge burial piles; imperious faces, all, gazing blindly and impassively into what eternities, what infinities, what unreturning oblivions?

Where the great prints had left their marks gouged deep into earth, he paused for a while, speculating dubiously as to what should be his course. The ocean surged ominously, and the southwest wind whooped harshly; and transitions of grayness alternated with gloom as the low wrack of clouds streamed across the high bank.

He set off toward Rano Raraku, following the huge holes that pitted the basalt at long intervals—colossal strides of what colossal agent! They had lost none of that forbidding aspect which had invested them the night before. If anything, their implications had grown more awesome. In the light of the gray day they produced, by their simple reality, a more vivid fear than the dreams that had haunted him during the hours he slept.

Graham experienced anew the depression of solitude; a loneliness emphasized by the violence of waters and the lash of wind; and now further intensified by the awareness that some agency unknown had made these pits. They reminded him of the little green statuette at Isling, and he wondered if the statuette had caused the deep rut as it came ashore, if it had then undergone a change, a metamorphosis into something else, and had walked up the slope in these great treads. It was a strange and frightening fancy, but no more strange than a universe which consisted of the inexplicable added to the incredible.

He strode on. The ground rose more steeply. The sea surged its endless requiem. Graham's face began to smart from the sting of particles of sand driven by the wind. At times he leaned against the gale, and looked at the sky. The high bank of cirro-cumulus clouds had moved on or dissolved into a uniform grayness. Far down on the western horizon a sinister black smudge had begun to mushroom.

Graham went on, over rocks and boulders, scrambling up steep ledges and crossing grass-plots. Here the haughty sculptures were fewer, but the line of pits continued, sinking deep into the basalt, pulverizing a mammoth boulder, or obliterating part of a rock ledge.

He continued following the pits toward Rano Raraku, and up its slopes to the cone, looking sharply around him as he crossed the sculptors' workshop. Completed and partly completed giants covered the outer slope of the volcano in what he considered the most awesome display on all earth. Many of the statues had fallen, yet they preserved their aspect of imperious and sovereign rule. A few vast heads, upright, looked as if they were emerging from the core of earth itself. Their eyes stared expressionless toward the ocean, facing land where land there was none for fifteen hundred miles. On what sunken continents had their gaze been fixed centuries ago? Or did they watch invisible worlds, awaiting the summons to life? The haughty countenances were those of a superior race, an alien race, a race of conquerors: the imperious brows, the downward-curving thin lips, the firm nose, these were the marks of their dominance. Mastery inhered in the gigantic stature of the figures, their bulking hugeness. A grotesque touch was added by the flat-backed heads which gave them a slanting angularity, suggestive of some queer system of geometry. Majestically looming erect, or lying where they had toppled, or partly buried in rubble, or tipping at a tangent, whatever their individual postures, singly and in mass they presented an aspect of outlandish and insensate superiority. This was more than the sculptors' workshop; it was a graveyard of the gods, a memorial mausoleum of anterior giants for all the ages.

The wind blew with still increasing force, eddies whirled against him, he heard the eternal dirge of seas that pounded afar. But even though he surveyed with quickened interest this riddle that he had not seen for more than a dozen years, he did not slacken his stride. The great holes continued beyond the great statues, and parrellel to their course he followed, past the area of giant figures and up the last slope to the rim of Rano Raraku where the pits disappeared beyond.

Perhaps Graham had speculated on what he might or

might not find; perhaps he had anticipated more, or less, than he discovered. The unreal reality before him swept all else away.

The crater of Rano Raraku spread below him much as he remembered it, but with a difference. For the lost image of greenish-gray material did indeed stand in the very center of the crater upon an enormous block of similar material, and the great holes he had been following ended before this altar. But it was not merely the re-discovery of the figurine that brought him to a halt. The statuette squatted evilly on its base, yet whirled through the malefic cycle of its transformations, a blur of energy and shifting outlines, from organism to metal to fluid to nightmare, from pygmy to titan to space run wild, curving and collapsing and surging through angles, solids, points, and extensions in the difficult geometry of a universe outside. It glowed with radiance of a color that did not appear in the spectrum. A baleful fire rippled into it and from it, a fire neither hot nor cold but painful because of its intensity, appalling in its nameless uniqueness. The idol emanated a spectral glow, the block underneath pulsed with the same indeterminate flux, and from both or toward both leaped a gigantic pillar of unearthly sheen upward and outward beyond the infinities of space. Graham's eyes ached as he peered overhead at this phenomenon, and saw how it pierced the clouds; and something constricted him as he noticed that the driving wrack could not close that gap. A force greater than nature as he knew it was at work. He sensed intuitively that the idol absorbed vigor and guidance across the abysses of space in that stream of baffling phosphorescence. Even while he looked, he detected a gradual thickening of the pillar, an intensifying of the unknown color, a wider range in the metamorphoses of the image.

Graham lurched unsteadily, struggling to regain his balance. What had happened? The sea thudded savagely, the wind whipped harder, but it was none of these. The whole island shuddered, and he felt the sickness of a wave akin to nausea. Would Easter Island sink? Other islands had gone down in the Pacific; and twice already he had experienced the heave of shaking earth. Yet there came never a waver in the glimmering pillar, nor the faintest sign of effect on the statuette; save that slowly and visibly the mutations broadened.

Graham walked forward, unwilling, yet fascinated by the shining flux. He slid down the inner slope, and stumbled to his feet on the ancient lava bed. The detritus of centuries had accumulated, leveling the base of the crater, but jagged scarps and sharp rocks protruding at intervals made walking difficult, as he advanced toward the altar, the figurine, and luminous pillar. The great column of fire completely circled the greenish block on which the idol rested, extending a dozen yards beyond it in all directions.

Graham halted at its fringe. Little more than arm's length from him, the color from space beyond emerged from the abysses above and ended on the dark, hard ground, terrifying in its magnitude, flowing from nowhere and ceasing at the strange little statuette. His eyes burned from the effect of this torturing sight: a new color behaving in an unpredictable manner, as far beyond radio-active rays as they are beyond ordinary fire. He saw the idol fluctuate through its cycle of transformations, so that he became almost hypnotized in trying to follow them. He could detect nothing of the purpose behind these forces in enormous action.

Tentatively, and with the chill of a mighty fear, he forced himself to reach out slowly, like the observer who sees a painted pole and is compelled to test its freshness. He expected a shock of some kind; he would not have been surprised, nor would he have cared, if that mysterious energy brought him instant and total destruction. But his reaching hand was neither burned nor irradiated. It stopped, pressing against a solid as impenetrable as a column of glass. He could no more force his way into the circle of that radiance than he could have pushed into the Dover cliffs. At the end of ten minutes, perspiring and numb with the nightmarish incongruity of it all, he gave up. And still the aching glow increased, the idol whirled incessantly, ever the wind skirled and the seas pounded.

And so Graham admitted defeat and returned to his camp. He took a pistol from his supplies, then retraced his steps to the crater of Rano Raraku. He had no expectation that bullets would alter the course of that towering and enigmatic flame, but he wanted to see the effect of the impact of matter in motion upon energy in action.

He felt a physical pressure, now, from the monotonous roaring of the sea, the maddening rush of the wind, the dark and gloomy skies, the loneliness and wildness.

During his absence, the phantasmal luminence had swelled, the figurine pulsated with more vital energy. Deliberately, and with care, he loaded the automatic. At such close range, it would have been nearly impossible for him to miss so huge a target, but he took aim as carefully as if he was participating in a match with experts. The automatic cracked sharply, and the splat of the striking bullet blended with the sound of the shot.

He could see no change whatever in the gyrating blur of the idol, no diminution in the color, not even a spark or flash of a minor explosion to indicate where the bullet had struck. He walked toward the continuing display of unearthly manifestation and halted at the edge of the fluid pillar. The flattened bullet lay at his feet. He stooped and held his hand near it. The bullet at least obeyed known laws; it was hot, from air friction and the impact.

But what known laws could possibly affect this alien stuff, this intruding element, this invader from outside? Explosives would be as useless as the bullet; in all probability, not even the theoretically absolute energies that could be liberated by nuclear fission would produce the slightest change in that apocalyptic presence. Nothing among known radiations was likely to pierce that impenetrable wall, but rather to be stilled or deflected. Nothing in the whole range of human scientific laws or available energies would apply to that new dynamism.

What could mortal do against the magic column?

And now Graham became aware of a reverberation that began to multiply in the air, like the echo of volcanos exploding at remote distances, or the drift of whole continents across the surface of earth, or the displacement of stars.

As if that tremendous sound was a signal, the column of radiant energy began to expand its radius with a slow and inexorable widening of the circle. The shining, ineffable, purposive light crept outward inch by inch, foot by foot, and as it flowed outward while the circle expanded, step by step Graham retreated before it. The flight of storm-clouds became a rout, the wind howled shrilly, the seas assaulted with fiercer attack the citadels of cliffs. The skies were shrouded with cyclonic black, and a thickness of murk obscured all Easter Island. But the endless tower of light palpitated, encroaching upon the barren spaces around. And in the heart of the baleful glare, the greenish idol flickered furiously through measureless vicissitudes of fluctuant being.

The living circle widened with a motion as dreadful as an artery responding to the beat of a pumping organism, sweeping outward, then drawing back a little, then surging farther afield. A luminous mist clouded the idol within, its outlines became vast, shadowy, an implacable will became expressed upon the altering features. To Graham it was more terrifying than would be a specter of death walking, with life persisting in an occupant of the grave. For this was beyond death and above life, exterior to knowledge; he was a mere atom, a primal grain of sand, in its overwhelming presence, as the topless pillar of indefinable fire throbbed and coursed while the image expressed its series of transmutations.

And ever the sentient column expanded, driving him back to the rim of the crater, and over its edge, and down the slopes of Rano Raraku, past the ancient sculptures. One by one, the imperious faces and the statues of the masters were swallowed within the circle; foot by foot the consuming cold fire followed after the fugitive, and always in that rhythmic arterial beat of advance and contraction, but each successive advance carrying farther and farther. Graham stared in a kind of entrancement as he backed toward the sea, retreating before the methodic march of the aggressive and expanding column. He could not even guess how or why the column stopped a bullet and rejected him, yet admitted the sculptures readily. Only a selective intelligence or a reason of intentional preference could have accounted for such a development; but selective intelligence in a living, phantasmal, energized, thickening column of unknown color was not for him to understand.

As the stone giants passed inside the pillar, a sinister and significant change occurred; they seemed to absorb the strange force with an automatic and natural thirst, as for a vital element long denied; and the color that was life breathed strongly into them and transformed them from hewn matter to the stir of awakening. Mobility came upon the great faces, and the sustenance reviving them was as the breath of creation upon rock, an animating compulsion on inert matter. The surging fire crept beyond them, and they moved mysteriously and deeper within, and assumed their relation to the shape that changed for ever as it guided the growth of the flame.

The world perished for Graham. Nothing existed but this enigma of time and space and power and matter and dominant will. The strain on his eyes grew intolerable, his head ached, his mind retreated into the past. He thought of the well at Isling. He had escaped from it. And this shaft, too, cleaving the skies above, like the shaft cleaving earth below, must obey, in its own realm and laws, a principle that would limit or control it just as a mechanism had launched it.

Back, ever back, down the outer slopes of Rano Raraku, and across the grass-covered shallows, Graham retreated, back to the cliffs and to the edge of mounting waters. The colossal tower of phosphorescence hung over the whole of Easter Island, pushing him beyond the jagged rocks, beyond the rings of burial platforms, to the beach.

N'ga n'ga rhthl'g clretl ust s g'lgggar—The sound superimposed itself on all other sound, the thunder of sea and the roaring gale and the blast of sheeted lightning.

Septhulchu nyrcg s thargoth k'tuhl s brogg—The cosmic chant came from infinitely far away, yet increasing rhythmically close to him. He thought of the Keeper of the Seal, of that eldritch figurine pulsing at the center of the measureless tower. He saw the pillar brighten until its baffling and blinding color burned with the incandescence of universes aflame, while the abominable image spun through its ultimate transformations. The pillar contracted, involuted to a vortex of multiple dimensions, became a link to other space and outer time. The flaming flux exceeded the range of sensory perception. Did the features of the statues emerge from the sleep of centuries and aeons? Did the breath of supersubstantial life animate the forms that had preceded mortality and now transcended the diuturnity of time? The titans returned, and the vast embodiments rippled, and the faces assumed the implacable, impersonal stare of other life. From other space and other time the titans entered through the door they had once opened, and closed, and now were opening again.

Meargoth s bh'rw'lutl ubcwthughu dägoth—This was the prophecy of their coming and the summons of the Keeper of the Seal. This was the fulfillment. Universe was linked to other space, worlds within and worlds without, and the master chemists from their alembic of galaxies and their laboratory in the ultracosmos returned to their experiment. In ways beyond comprehension they bridged trillions of light-years in moments, contracted their forms into the core of that atom which was Graham's universe.

And now every stone sculpture was a strange life, an inscrutable life, as hundreds upon hundreds they ringed the symbol figurine that had given them being, the Keeper of the Seal. The circle of titans was only less than the circle of mystical flame, and the flame was only less than the inhabitants descending from other space and other time. And ring upon ring the great ones returned and the carved

ones arose for whatever purpose was theirs, beyond conjecture. The pillar was a maelstrom of corrupt color, fogs
of somber splendor irradiated its length, it burned in an
amorphous vortex of all the strangeness of all the unknown realm outside. And the stony giants stood with
the weird pallor of their new life hazing their faces, and a
glimmering misty luminence drifting around them; and
the masters, the great chemists, loomed in the flame, expanding even as the statuette had expanded illimitably,
and vacillating through cycles of eternal change.

The time was come; and Graham thought of the old
Sekhite and the passage he had read from antique archives:

*When the stars are come to the positions prophesied
and fixed in the pattern prescribed, then will the titans
awaken and return. Earth shall open. Out of crypts
deeper than the clouds are high shall the Keeper of the
Seal issue forth a summons to the titans. The Keeper
of the Seal shall become even as the titans and take his
place on Crltul Thr. The waters shall boil, the earth
shall split, the lightnings break and the skies burn.
From their plane outside the stars shall the titans
descend. All life shall be claimed by them who fashioned us from the dust that quickened and the fire
that consumed. These things shall come to pass when
the titans awaken when the stars are set, lest there
come he who challenges the Keeper of the Seal with
the secret of secrets. If he challenge the Keeper, and if
he succeed, then shall the Keeper return unto stone
and the titans wait until the great sphere of stars shall*

reach again the position predetermined. And the Keeper of the Seal shall remain on the axis from Crltul Thr to Mrcg.

Graham listened, waiting and ready to challenge, in the only manner that might conceivably prove effective.

The syllables resounding through the atmosphere from the difficult vocalisms of the Keeper had ceased. But while the sound still quivered in turbulent echos, Graham spoke other sounds of other values, in a kind of rolling chant, spoke a gibberish of unfamiliar phrases to the Keeper, flung the answer to its own cryptic utterances, but with a difference; whatever difference existed between the characters on the upper half of the Seal at Isling and the glyphics on its lower half. For Graham had reasoned that the auditory expression of the first group controlled and set in motion through some abstruse mechanism the obscure laws of the phenomenon he witnessed; and that the second sequence might logically be the key that would prevent those forces from becoming wholly realized, the key that might suspend them, a key provided by the titans themselves to the Keeper of the Seal if the need for it arose, through circumstances unplanned.

Graham had memorized those symbols the previous night, his lips moving silently as he went over and over again Professor Alton's reconstruction of their sound. He knew that there was nothing else within human comprehension or experience to employ against these entities; only their own discoveries could combat them, only the extranormal could counter the extranormal.

He did not know what the sounds meant, or if they had
a meaning, according to human concepts; he did not know
the principle of their operation. His only approximation
to understanding their principle was to think of them as a
kind of complex tuning-fork in audible series, a series
that affected the pattern of the greenish image, and through
its pattern was multiplied and delivered to that greater
and remoter pattern outside, causing instant actions and
changes, realignments and inversions.

As the last syllables sounded, Graham saw convulsion
riot through the living pillar of mind. The column surged
over him, encompassing him, selecting him, absorbing him
within the framework and the laws of its alien existence.

He felt the disruptions of massive tension and torsion
and vortex, pressure and vacuum, integration and disintegration. He walked in time, and withdrew from space.
He approached the titans, but they were gone. He drifted
in energies so blindingly bright that he perceived shining
blackness. Stars were spinning through him, as he extended
on the beat of an absolute pulse.

XII

THE DREAM

ALL day long, under the dusky glare of a green sun that flamed across the somber sky, he had been traversing a burnt and blackened waste in his search. All day he had been crossing a dead and utterly lifeless land, and when the green sun set he had not yet emerged from it. But even as the sun set, with its dying emerald glow it had lit darkly for a moment a forest of some sort far ahead. Toward it he went.

Night deepened around him as the sun sank from a strange twilight to a darkness, and from the darkness to an ebony blackness that crouched upon the land, but he did not pause. Onward he travelled toward the forest, guided by faint and unfamiliar constellations of stars that burned coldly and whitely in the sky above.

For a long time he kept on through thick darkness, ever pressing toward that forest ahead, and it was only when he had gone more than half-way that the darkness lightened dimly when a huge, blood-red moon swept up from the eastern sky and cast a livid, leprous glow on the land. In tremendous bounds it fled across the sky, surrounded by a many-colored rout of streaming satellites. The air hung heavy and listless, and in the unearthly light of the red sun seemed to be oozing with a myriad globules of blood. The land, burnt before, took on a desolation and an aspect

of solitude as if a red rot were creeping through its rocks
and sand.

He continued onward, and had almost reached the
forest when the rushing red sun sank with all its satellites.
But from every side, from each of the distant horizons, a
horde of twisting comets rocketed up, and the suffering
vault became alive with jagged streaks of light hurtling
erratic and aimless from horizon to horizon.

Dank and dark loomed the forest; right and left it
stretched in never-ending line until it faded and vanished
in distant glooms. The wanderer plunged forward. In a
moment he was threading his way through gigantic trees
that towered up and up. The darkness deepened steadily
as the branches of trees interlocked more and more closely,
until the entire sky was hidden from his sight and the
sullen branches formed a solid roof high overhead. He
picked his way in and out through gaunt white trunks,
strangely like tombstones and bearing fantastic inscriptions, that rose around him, and all the while that he
moved forward they became thicker and thicker. Creepers
began to make their appearance. From every side of the
black forest he heard things chuckling in the darkness; ever
and again faint whisperings reached him, and sometimes
he saw shadows peering from behind the tree-boles. The
still air was pregnant with a thousand sounds of sibilant
whispers moaning through the forest.

But he pressed onward, always before his eyes a vision of
the lithe and slender loveliness of his lost Iris. The creepers
thickened and thickened until he had to claw his way past

them, until, finally, he drew forth the great green-bladed sword with curiously carven hilt that hung at his side and hacked his way through. And every creeper that he slashed shrieked aloud, and from the severed ends dripped a soft, warm substance. . . . The forest became suddenly malignant and malefic. The baleful creepers twined insidiously about his legs, and all along his path the wounded ones howled in swelling ululations that made the forest echo with waves of fiendish sound. Thick vines clutched at him like the trailing talons of some huge and hairy arm. And when he cut them, they wailed like flayed children. . . . He lunged ahead faster, and the branches whipped at him. His face grew scratched and bloody from the flailing of branches that ripped his shirt and flesh and that twined around him. He beat them off and staggered onward.

Suddenly the ground underfoot grew damp. He halted just in time. For in front of him, stretching away until it vanished in the night ahead and on either side, lay a vast, slimy slough. The forest came down to its very edge, and even throughout it, here and there, stood gaunt, dead trees, and in places half-submerged logs rotted. As far as he could look to his right and left, the swamp spread its interminable length. He debated for a moment; he looked again at the logs, the stumps, and the occasional unfallen trees that rose at intervals. Then he decided to risk it, and ran forward.

The going was easy for a time. He walked across great tree trunks lying in ooze, or jumped from stump to stump, or swam through patches of stagnant water covered by a luminous green slime. Sometimes he dragged himself through mud that made a husky, sucking sound when he pulled out his legs, like the sound of some enormous witch that smacked her lips. On one or two occasions, it seemed to him that a shadow passed overhead, a sweeping shadow as of a huge nocturnal thing. . . . He shuddered as he stumbled onward.

He came to an open space, brown-covered. Unthinking, he plunged in and swam. The entire surface instantaneously lived with a million million wriggling shapes that swarmed in hellish motion. Hissing snakes moved from his path and piled up on each side; cold vipers slithered across his back and neck, squirming like fat worms in a carcass. He dived under the surface and swam as long as he could. When he rose, the water was moving with mounting waves of serpents, and great bunches of snakes threshed on every side. The affrighted air trembled in one mighty hiss that ascended from the hordes.

When at last the water ended in mud and he pulled himself up on a rotting log, he lay for a long while regaining his strength. The seething mass of reptiles gradually subsided, and when he resumed his way was quiescent. Above, the comets had fled from the sky, and the heavens were void and absolutely empty in a terrible blackness.

Hour after hour he ploughed through foul swamps and slimy water. The noisome odors of the place made him dizzy after a time, but he fought onward. He occasionally thought of casting away the sword which hung heavy and cumbersome at his side, but he kept it. He knew not what he might encounter.

He must have travelled for leagues before he staggered

from the slough unexpectedly. He was on firm ground, but the forest had ceased. He lay down on the earth for a while to rest his weary body, and carelessly looked back across the slough. From far behind came a shuddering heave; as he watched, something gigantic and horrible rose out of the depths and mounted upward. At the top of the soaring bulk he saw a head swaying from side to side with one huge central eye gleaming blindly.

In a moment he had leaped to his feet and was trotting forward until the slough and the monster were entombed in the deepening gloom behind.

The ground was level and covered with a tall grass or reed that rustled gently. And a soft night wind began to arise in fitful moans and whisper with the grass in a reedy rustling. The melancholy music came dim from the sounding darkness, infinitely somber and plaintive, in strange, minor harmonies and lonely chanting as if the drooping soul of misery itself were floating through the reeds. From every side as he passed came, low and elusive, the rhythmic cadences, a mournful litany from the whispering grass. All the plain seemed weeping at his passing, and he became filled with a desire to rush through the trackless extent and soothe the crying of the grass. But there rose before his eyes the shadowy, haunting beauty of his Iris: in one fearful second the sounds blended together and streamed in speeding waves to the utmost darkness. And the plain was as a thing that, having lived, had died.

Winding and tortuous his way became, shortly afterward, when the plain ceased abruptly near a range of hills. And even as he entered them, the darkness again began to lighten. By the time he had crossed the hills, a wan, immense moon was crossing the sky like a decaying thing that fled, shunned by the aloof, ebon depths of the heavens. It cast a pallor, sick and deathly, on the ground; it limned the gaunt trees pallidly against the sky; it laid a soft and fat covering of white rottenness on everything it touched. And under the ghastly paleness the wanderer's features took on the appearance of a walking corpse. A nameless fear began to creep through him, and he went on faster toward the mountains towering beyond the hills. An utter solitude and silence had settled over the dreary waste. The country the traveler had crossed crouched faintly luminous far behind, but he turned not. Once he looked at the vault above, but the entire concameration was completely and desolately empty of all save blackness and that westward-waning moon. Only the steady low fall of his steps broke the appalling silence; all things that lay on every side as far as he could see conspired to give him a sense of minuteness in an infinitude that extended, ceaseless, upward and outward through the vacua overhead.

And as the wanderer mounted the trail that was now winding through the base of the mountains, the rocks and trees in some indescribable way began to absorb the light that fell on them, until they moved stealthily in slow corruption. And as he continued, it seemed to him that they changed their positions . . . as if to block his path. He touched a stone. A shiver of fear ran through him, for the stone was living . . . panting like some monstrous toad. In

a sudden anger, he grasped his sword and smote the rock.
It was cleft, so that the halves fell apart. And even as the
sword touched it, the rock shrieked. From its core poured
forth a horde of worms. . . . And the rocks began to converge toward him, like crawling heaps of liquescence, and
the trees began to walk. Gasping, he slashed about him.
He could do nothing. Wet, cold things were gathering
around his feet and creeping up his legs. . . . Dead horrors
caressed his flesh. . . . And in his despair, he thought of Iris:
there came to his mind the picture of her slim, willowy
body, and half-shut dreaming eyes. . . .

With a start, he came to himself. The rocks and trees
were still and lifeless. The moon had sunk with all its pale
deathliness.

He resumed his progress, and discovered that he was
ascending an easy grade to the last of the foothills. He
emerged upon its top to find before him a gently rounded
plateau in the midst of which stood a city of sepulture.
There was no way of encircling it, for the unaccountably
paved road that he walked on ran straight through its heart,
nor could he see any other path which he might take.
Without pausing, he continued to walk forward, his steps
falling mechanically.

It was a city of overwhelming strangeness. Its fantastic
spires fretted a raven-colored sky, and all the thousands of
buildings beneath, even as they, were monoliths and ceno-
taphs and obelisks, devoid of windows or doors. He went
unchallenged. The inhabitants, if the city was ever occupied, had mysteriously perished, leaving behind them

only their sepulchral architecture gradually to crumble and dissolve. It somehow seemed natural that vanished hands had engraved upon them a counterpart of the cryptic legend scrolled on the hilt of his sword. He longed for a face he knew, or a familiar sound out of the lost years: he saw a ruinous city of death, heard his steps echo hollowly away among deserted aisles and corridors. The inertness of stone mocked him, and he unsheathed his sword, cursing the solitudes that had entrapped him. And the city submerged in the ground. He traversed a bleak and barren plateau.

For hours he wandered on. The path steadily rose and wound upward through tremendous mountains that towered on every side. Darkness reigned, but the path lay distinct.

It was only when he had ascended nearly to the top of the central range that the gloom again lightened. Ahead of him loomed a cup-shaped circle of giants over which hung a faint and almost impalpable phosphorescence that illuminated slightly the grandeur of stupendous and colossal peaks. But he paused not to survey the scene; he followed the path where it led through a rift in the cup to the hollow itself.

The phosphorescence shimmered everywhere, and, as he passed, seemed to be thickening. The air suddenly and indescribably became fraught with expectation. It was as if his arrival were awaited.

When he reached the center of the cup, he stopped on the margin of a pit that blocked his way; and when he stopped, there came a change. The slow-drifting phosphorescence leaped into life and rushed toward the mountainous walls in one cataclysmic surge. There the sweeping luminosity collected and condensed, and around him in a great circle sprang up a low, running line of flame. In a moment the circle was completed and the light rose upward. Almost before he could move, a solid wall of cold radiance burned about him, mounting in immense waves.

And all the light was flame; and all the flame was gold.

And now there began to come a sound, a faint sound as of the moan of distant waters, while higher, higher, higher mounted the liquid waves of light around the circle.

And all the light was flame, and all the flame was red.

And the distant moaning came louder and louder, rising in the ever-growing roar of mighty, warring seas. The light began to converge in a funnel-shaped roof above his head, drawing after it the thicker waves.

And all the light was flame; and all the flame was green.

A titanic wash filled the air alive in quickening motion, and a thunderous roar as of all the billion billion waters of all the worlds boomed with a space-annihilating crash of sundering stars toward the funnel. And the sheeted flame above commenced a spinning motion until it whirled furiously and dizzily in a twisted wrack of shifting radiance.

And all the light was flame; and all the flame was black.

Abysmal storms howled toward the funnel in roar on deafening roar. The funnel widened and lengthened suddenly and swept apart to form a maelstrom around an immense vacancy that led to outer space. Far overhead, the blackness of the sky moved and streamed in mighty rivers of ebon that serpentined madly toward the funnel.

He stood dazed and deafened by the fearful thunder of space-leaping winds and the uncontrollable forces lashing themselves to savage fury all around. Instinctively he tried to cry out, but no word issued from his lips.

The flame flung itself together in a coalescing bound. It soared zenithward, one huge, solid pillar of fire. He followed its lengthening, already league-long, height far above. It seemed to him that a greater glare gathered at its peak, and that something had formed there.

Again he strove in vain to cry out.

All the howling winds poured downward and fled in hurtling rout around the pillar of flame, walling it with a speeding blackness. He tried to move but was powerless. There was the briefest tension, the pillar became motionless in subdued gales, as if expectant, and *they* were waiting —waiting—

But he remained helplessly immobile.

The tower of flame which had hung still for a moment leaped outward toward the eternal blackness. Thundering, screaming winds swept vengefully down and about him. He was torn by a million waters fighting, smashing, and the noise of all enormous seas burst through his ears. He stumbled forward toward the pit, battered by angry, pounding tempests. His arms waved wildly, he clutched for support, slipped, and now at last found his voice and cried aloud, too late, bitterly too late. His sole answer was mounting winds that raced away after the flying pillar of flame. Incredibly distant already he saw the living stream of fire that rocketed mockingly into space. He was whirled and twisted in the after-suction of the blasts, all around was a jetty infinitude of shouting darkness that hurtled in the flame's wake.

His futile cries were drowned, there answered him only the sardonic, gusty mirth of vanishing hurricanes, the hiss of a measureless sea that washed farther and farther distant, the dying echo of a cosmic whisper that faded into nothingness.

Down, down, he plunged through the pit, points of light flashed by him like stars, worlds and universes swam from sable below and were erased in blackness above. Each second was an aeon, eternity was an instant, time and space had swallowed him, down, down.

He abruptly wakened from his dreaming reverie, and found himself in the midst of desert wasteland. A green sun was crawling over the horizon and bathing him in its necrophilic glare. Wearily he resumed his quest.

He knew that all day long, under the dusky glare of a green sun that flamed across the somber sky, he would traverse a burnt and blackened wasteland in his quest. For nothing lay behind him; and all the hideous way was yet to be travelled.

XIII

THE WEB

THE phenomena attending the partial entry of the titans, his challenge, and the surge of more than cosmic forces that overwhelmed him, Graham could remember. But afterwards—

The strangest sense of suspended animation came upon him. The world wavered and retreated beyond mist. A shadowy vast gulf enfolded him. Time ceased. He had no consciousness of space or being. He lost all trace of identity for the briefest yet most eternal of seconds. The titans had vanished, weirdly, as they had come. He had challenged them, and he had won. Yet he had no feeling of triumph. A pregnant unease, a great doubt, possessed him. And that phantom mid-region of inertia in which he was cloudily trapped—was it the vortex of the flame and the link floating free between his universe and that which was outside? The flux where time and space united with multiple dimensions and mysterious powers in the laws of that greater existence, whose workings enveloped him but which he could neither clearly perceive nor understand? He moved and yet was unable to move, felt the drift of tremendous alien energies but was powerless; his very life and mind seemed to have been caged in an intangible prison, and his body stolen from any realm in which to exist. He swayed like a weed in the grip of green ocean-currents, borne slowly and for ever across wide expanses.

Always there was a drone in his ears, and a curtain of haze before his eyes, and particles of fire like stars, but cold, whirling in confusion through him. And then these all died away, and there was blankness. And in this blankness a vivid dream took form, a dream in which he wandered alone amidst wastelands, a nightmare that grew with steady, persistent, cumulative horror. Then the dream faded into blankness again, and the blankness extended itself, lengthening beyond time.

Then Graham began to assemble the scattered fragments of his identity, as though they fled back to him from afar. The return of awareness was accompanied by a puzzling thought, the feeling that he had slipped off the beat of some unimaginable pulse and drifted away like a note from a cosmic musical scale.

He had a sensation of falling from a great height, and for a long time. And then cold water soaked him, and he opened his eyes after the shock of immersion, and found himself struggling on the surface of a moderately quiet sea, with the light of day around him. He saw a speck in the heavens that grew larger, and dropped toward him. He watched it with curiosity, but no elation at the prospect of rescue. An extreme lassitude gripped him, and he accepted without wonder the fact that no trace of Easter Island or any island rose from the sea.

The speck came to rest, complete rest, a hundred yards overhead. It hung there with no visible support or principle of suspension. He thought what an odd looking craft it was. There were no motors that he could observe, yet it was larger than the greatest airship he had ever before seen. In shape it somewhat resembled the diamond on a playing card, while its skin was of some thin, opaque material the hue of amber.

A door opened in its side, and a man stepped out and walked toward Graham. Graham watched this uncanny sight with a new amazement, inadvertently swallowing a gulp of salt water that set him to coughing violently. The man continued descending through the air as though he walked down an invisible staircase. He was a figure of grotesque appearance, with an oversize head, a shrivelled body, spidery limbs, and big, deep eyes.

And then he stood directly above Graham, and spoke in soft, liquid words that had the trill-like quality of a bird's song. They resembled no speech or language that Graham had ever heard. He thought dazedly that he must have emerged on a remote world at the utmost end of the fluid pillar. He shook his head as best he could, floating on his back in the water. The stranger looked astonished. Graham called to him in English, then a few phrases he knew of other languages—Spanish, German, French, Italian, even Latin and Siamese, a little imperfect Arabic and some Chinese that he had accumulated during his years of exploration. But the stranger poised in air only looked more puzzled at Graham floating on the calm sea. Finally the stranger stepped down with the same assurance as before of descending a staircase and offered Graham his hand.

Graham smiled. He began to feel light-headed. It was all an amusing fantasy, but he could end it quickly. He lifted a wet arm from the water and grasped the outstretched hand. He was shocked to find it real. He was more bewildered than ever when this frail creature lifted him easily, pulled him from the water, and walked up the stairway of air back to the oddly shaped craft. Graham laughed at the absurdity of it; the tensions and storms and drains on his vitality sought relief in a burst of mirth. The pleasure of floating skyward was not to be denied. The grotesque gnome looked at him gravely, curiously, with a query in his large, deep eyes.

He drew Graham into the stationary aircraft. Impressions began to crowd so rapidly upon Graham, then, that they tended to blur. He saw many more of these grotesque people, and the women were virtually identical with the men, having the same flat chest, the same hairless heads, the same spindly structure.

His guide led Graham to a chamber where he exchanged his wet clothing for new garments, a kind of tunic made from material with a metallic bronze sheen, though soft and warm. Graham became aware of hunger, and made an obvious gesture. His host brought him small plastic phials filled with liquids of various hues. He drank several of them. They had pleasant tastes that he did not recognize; but immediately he felt sustenance reviving him, and his senses grew keener. Whatever the liquids were, they acted more swiftly than foods that he knew.

The quick response to his gesture of being hungry

showed the way to the only method of establishing communication. Graham would point to an object and name it, then the grotesque creature would name it, and so, arduously, they built up a small vocabulary of nouns. It was much harder to identify verbs, but they succeeded in solving simple ones, like "walk", "eat", "write", "speak", and so on. The written symbols that Graham saw on various screens and recording tapes were as unfamiliar as the words he heard. They seemed to be a kind of shorthand for a highly advanced phonetic script.

In the meantime, the craft had resumed its flight; the navigator pressed a few simple dials; and apparently without further attention, the ship rose and winged its way toward its destination which, judging by the position of the sun, lay somewhere northeast.

The other occupants surveyed Graham with as much surprise as he exhibited for them; and just as he found their garb exotic, with its tunic lines and the abundance of attached mechanical devices, so they regarded him as though he was something totally foreign or utterly extinct.

Uneasiness increased in Graham; the spindly people, their bird-like language and trillings, the meaningless objects that adorned them, and the bizarre craft, all exemplified the vast gulf between their world and his.

Graham had learned that the stranger who rescued him was called Moia Tohn. Graham took one of the writing instruments and drew a quick chart of the solar system. He pointed to the sun in the sky, named it, and pointed to the sun on the chart. He indicated the earth with a sweep of his arm, named it, and pointed to earth on the chart. Thus he established recognition of the solar system, and discovered that he was indeed still on earth; but now he grew baffled again. He launched a new line of inquiry, to determine the year or date; here, however, the difficulties of communication were very great, and concepts of time hard to express by visual gesture.

Moia Tohn now consulted with one of the other passengers; a reluctant agreement was reached by them; and Moia Tohn, with an expression of regret as though he was about to subject Graham to a great indignity, led him to a chamber with a screen and a chair that had an attached cap with many wires. He placed the cap on Graham's head; and Graham stared at the screen in amazement, for the pictures in his mind became visualized on the screen. He thought of Iris; and Iris was there. Moia Tohn also looked on, with symptoms of unusual excitement. But Graham, depressed by the image, let the screen go blank.

He found, by experimenting, that thoughts and concepts, abstract emotions and ideas did not translate to the screen. But any visual picture did. And after a moment of the old regret, Graham suppressed the memory of Iris. He had a message for these people; and they needed an explanation for him. He concentrated his attention; and he presented, not all, but selected sequences of the events that brought him to Easter Island; and even he watched with a shiver as he saw again that ravenous column of aggressive energy from outside.

Then Moia Tohn seated himself. And Graham saw, on

the screen, a view of empty ocean. Suddenly a great pillar, vague, misty, ghostlike, made a brief appearance and was gone, but in the water threshed a mote of man who had materialized from nowhere and fallen from a point at the base of the momentary column.

So that was it, Graham thought; the return of the pillar, and his exit from it, had been witnessed; his rescue followed.

Graham now attempted the more difficult problem of finding out what year it was. He indicated the concept of time by visualizing the sun crossing the screen swiftly, to be succeeded by an instant of star-covered darkness and the moon, then the sun rising again. He showed, also, the great column engulfing him on Easter Island, and the numerals of the year in which he had vanished.

Moia understood, and looked stunned. He gravely seated himself, and through pictorial development informed Graham that not within living memory had there been land in the vicinity, and that he had never heard of Easter Island or its statues. He then transferred to the screen a symbol meaningless to Graham; a mathematical symbol which he went on to interpret as his indicator for the current year, by placing beneath it the approximate numerical equivalent of that symbol; and now Graham was stunned. For this was the year 1,500,000, more or less.

The year one million, five hundred thousand! Not an exact figure, for Moia Tohn was evidently on unfamiliar ground in trying to reduce his mathematical symbol to its precise equation in calendar years as Graham would count them. But what would a few centuries or a thousand centuries matter?

He had leaped one and one-half million years into the future. That journey across time explained the grotesque changes which had occurred in man, as shown by Moia Tohn and the other occupants of the airship; it explained the liquid new language, the marvels of technological advance; but it left Graham a freak, an intrusion of the primitive into a world of complex maturity.

Graham felt the need for a respite from all thinking, an interval in which to adjust himself to the shock of this revelation. But before he left the chamber, Moia Tohn, who had been watching him, took the seat again and remained seated as Graham went out. In this manner, Graham learned that the wonderful mechanism, a triumph of technical genius, had no practical value to these people. They used it as a toy, a plaything, a device for individual recreation and self entertainment. And it was because of the low regard that they held for the mind-screen that Moia Tohn had consulted with a companion before subjecting Graham to the indignity of baring his private mind to others even for the purposes of communication.

During a long period, then, Graham fell into a gloomy fit of abstraction, staring moodily through a cabin window. He was mentally fatigued to the point of exhaustion, if not collapse. The strain of this succession of nightmarish experiences overburdened his mind; and this fantastic aftermath, this bridging of fifteen hundred thousand years, fifteen thousand full centuries, in a single night of oblivion, stunned him into a kind of apathy. He shrank from facing the great changes that must have occurred in the world during his absence. The marvels of science that he had already witnessed were mere commonplaces, elementary needs, even playthings, to these people; ahead of him must lie profundities of thought, miracles of intellectual achievement, pinnacles of material, social, and artistic accomplishment for the increased welfare, happiness, and knowledge of all men. The secrets of the atom, cosmic radiation, and the galactic universe, of medical research and biological determination, of interplanetary travel, problems upon which the scientists of Graham's age had been working, must long since have been solved. It was not inconceivable that life and death could now be stated as exact formulas, under precise laboratory control.

Thus drowsing, Graham fell asleep, a deep and heavy slumber from which he did not awaken for more than twenty hours.

When he arose the following day, he found that he had been taken off the aircraft and placed in a spheroid house, suspended from a central tube, quarters assigned to him by the world council. Moia Tohn was there, also, having been delegated to give Graham all the aid he needed in understanding the structure of civilization, and in assuming his place in it. The process was one that might well continue for the entire balance of his life; but Graham sought only a general grasp of what had happened on earth during his absence. He had reason to believe that everything he wanted to know must be learned within the next few days.

He discovered that a world records office kept a tally on

each individual from birth to death. His arrival had created a minor sensation, for there was nothing to indicate that he had ever existed. Moia Tohn took the necessary data from him to initiate his tally in the records office.

Graham's first request was for a map of the world. Moia Tohn led him to a branch of the records office.

The global map that Graham studied showed vast changes from the geography he remembered. There was no London. Most of England had sunk beneath the encroaching sea. Only Ireland, part of Scotland, and a tip of Wales remained as three small islands. He looked at them sadly, thinking of his friends; all dead and gone for oblivious years beyond reach; all his customary haunts vanished, all his possessions and the places he knew lost without hope of contact. He could never again visit the land of his birth. He saw that the Japanese Isles, also, were no more, that a new sea had formed where the Sahara desert once lay, and that a new continent nearly as large as Australia had risen in the south Atlantic. Everywhere old coasts had altered, old lands had sunk, new lands had emerged from the depths of the oceans. He was a Crusoe who could not rejoin his people, a Rip Van Winkle whose awakening came from a past of such remote antiquity that it carried no meaning to even the wisest of living men.

That day, and thereafter, Graham paid little attention to the curious foods that were served as meals, though they looked like concentrates and extracts. He never attempted to learn the principle by which men now walked through air at will. He supposed it to involve the operation of a counter-force to gravity. He did not take the trouble to find out how the airplanes—and of these he saw great numbers in the sky, and of many bizarre torpedo, disc, and cone shapes—were propelled, though he surmised that atomic energy might have been used, or direct power from sub- and super-cosmic rays. He neither knew nor cared about the details of technology and invention.

He spent days, with Moia Tohn's help, in the records office, surveying basic trends through the ages that he had missed. Wars and famines ceased by the thirtieth century. The era of interplanetary exploration, and later of galactic travel, lasted beyond the hundredth century, until final determination that life existed nowhere except on earth.

A period of glaciation came, with a sharp decrease in the population of the world; and a thousand centuries later, the arrival of a cosmic cloud, a gaseous cloud, that killed everyone except a few hundred men and women in different parts of the world who happened to be in enclosures under water, such as submarines, diving bells, and marine studios. From these scattered units began a new struggle to survive, a period of hundreds of centuries of the twilight of knowledge before the progress of the race resumed. And again came cataclysm in the form of a small comet that collided with earth, once more nearly obliterating man, and causing most of the changes he had observed in the earth's surface.

Now, in this year of Moia Tohn, a single race inhabited earth; a race that was a blend of all the colors and nations that Graham had known, a race of golden-bronze hue, the final admixture of white man and black, red man and yellow and brown. They spoke a single language, the bird-like trilling of Moia Tohn, and were organized into a single world-state. The life-span was approximately one thousand years. The control of atomic and other energies had produced such abundance that virtually no work was required of man, except to supervise the operation of machines. Birth was no longer a family matter; the family unit had not existed for thousands of centuries. The world council determined how many births should occur, selected the mothers, and artificially inseminated them. The children were brought up under the direction of the council, on specialized diets and for specialized duties. It was this disappearance from women of nursing as a function that had resulted in organic atrophy, and the gradual deterioration of the breast until women now exhibited the same flat chest that men had.

But while the life-span was now a thousand years, few individuals attained it. In every community stood a chamber, provided by the world council, where those who grew weary of living, or bored with knowledge, could enter and end their lives voluntarily, with pellets of exquisite taste that drifted the visitor off on waves of ineffable pleasure. The community in which Graham had taken temporary residence lay near Bear Mountain overlooking the sea that covered Long Island, Manhattan, and the old Hudson valley. Moia-Tohn led him to the local Tower of Departure, a cylinder of glass a thousand feet tall with a sky dome like the cap of a mushroom. In this lofty retreat, looking down upon a broad panorama of earth and ocean, the fugitive from life could make his exit with a magnificent view of all that he abandoned.

Even the vegetation that Graham looked down on from that high dome had changed; for the botanists had developed mutations of trees and flowers far different from those that Graham remembered; just as the technicians in medical research had helped to alter the structure of man by eliminating disease and all harmful germs and viruses; and as social evolution had altered the structure of civilization by blending the races and eliminating the family unit, by the practice of artificial insemination and laboratory controlled breeding which reduced sex from a once powerful force to an unimportant and uninteresting aspect of life.

Graham asked how frequently the facilities of the Tower of Departure were used. He learned that in this community called Nuaya, with a population of 8,000, the voluntary exits averaged one every thirty days. During the past two days, however, nine individuals had ascended the Tower. Graham nodded absently. The increase was what he had expected, what he feared.

The following morning, Graham attempted to grasp the fundamental premises, the laws and applications, of the new mathematics. He thought that an understanding of them might help him greatly in his efforts to explain what had happened to him during his absence in the great pillar of alien energy. The new mathematics, however, was so abstract, so far advanced even from the level of Einstein, Whitehead and Russell, that he realized he would never comprehend it. It was based on five dimensions; to length, breadth, thickness, and time, a fifth dimension called Ru had been added. Graham not only did not learn the laws of the five-dimensional mathematics; he did not succeed in obtaining more than a vague notion about the dimension called Ru. For Ru, as a tool for measurement like the other dimensions, differed from them in being of itself measureless; it was a fluctuation, a changeable, representing the continuous mutability of observer, object, and universe each in relation to the other. Farther than this Graham could not follow; decades of study might provide him the background for understanding, but he did not even have days remaining, if his fears were correct.

For Graham had had a terrifying dream the night before, of the titans returning through the link from their realm to this universe, just as they had started to enter on Easter Island that evening fifteen thousand centuries before. He had dreamed of the awesome idol, and the corrupt flame, and the insufferable color, and the fluid, living, aggressive pillar of energized mind.

In the late afternoon, Graham walked to the Tower of Departure. It did not surprise him to count four men and women who ascended the Tower during the period while he watched. None of them returned. The sight depressed him. Only abnormal circumstances could cause so many of these gravely wise, long-lived, and tolerant people to extinguish their existence, as if the desire for departure had suddenly spread like a contagion.

Graham slept badly that night, and wakened in the grip of a black melancholy, a mood of despair. It was a sultry, windless day of breathless heat at summer's end. He awoke from another nightmare, concerning a search that involved laborious climbing *downward*, miles upon miles, forcing his way through a resistant darkness like soft and yielding earth. After aeons of this delving he broke into nighted vaults of infinity, where the dead drifted in slow rhythms, and bright living ones fell among them, and a glimmer of green phosphorescence began to form whirls and whorls and glowing cryptoglyphics of prophecy; till eternity became a flame, and infinity a devouring shadow, and the tide of living and dead rushed away in a vast ebb that swept Graham toward some dreadful ultimate that he constantly approached but never reached, and yet from which he could never retreat.

He dressed and went walking along the sea shore for relief from the dream, but heat rose in waves from the sand and a glare of sun burned dazzling off the water. The slight breeze blowing inland felt humid and sticky. He could not shake off the weight of his fears, nor could he accept them as truth.

The direction of his steps changed; and he found himself passing the Tower of Departure. During the few minutes that the entrance at the base of the Tower remained in sight, he saw several Nuayans go in; their features preserved their habitual calmness and repose, without a trace of emotion. They were of all ages, from youths of one hundred to mature men of four and five hundred to old women of eight or nine hundred years. The big, deep eyes, so sage in their gaze, affected Graham strongly. He had come to respect what had at first seemed to him a paradox of their existence: they possessed a highly developed sense of racial unity, but they also displayed a great respect for the privacy of individual mind. Thus Graham did not know what motives impelled the visitors to the Tower; and he could not insult them by questioning them.

He returned to his quarters in order to concentrate his attention on a miraculous machine which he had hitherto ignored. This product of inventive genius was the unitel, a device installed in every residence throughout the world. It bore a distant kinship with radio and television as he had known them, but perfected and extended. The unitel consisted essentially of a viewing screen, a sealed box containing the operating mechanism, and a grid bearing a map of the world, with a selector needle under enormous magnification. By adjusting the selector needle and closing a contact, Graham could reproduce on the screen whatever was occurring in any area of the earth, in full colors and with every sound, every motion, every change. Once a day, for thirty minutes, the world council blanketed all unitel sets with an accounting for its activities and decisions, with information and news of general interest. At all other times the unitel would operate as the individual chose.

Graham found the official transmission in progress, and listened intently.

All over the world, there had come a sharp rise in the numbers resorting to the Towers of Departure. The world capital, the largest of all communities, a city with a population of 30,000 in the Andean approaches of what had once been Brazil, reported forty-one exits in one day compared to its statistical average of nineteen one-hundredths, or .19, daily. Other localities showed similar increases.

Graham did not understand many passages in the council spokesman's report, for he had only a rudimentary knowledge of the new language. He did, however, catch an allusion to a phenomenon taking place over ocean waters; if the location was given, he missed that detail also. But he did not need it; only one small area of earth could produce a phenomenon of a kind that would substantiate his fears.

He waited until the spokesman ended her official report, when the unitel automatically reverted to individual control. He then closed the contact and began moving the selector needle toward the south Pacific. As the needle moved, he glanced at the screen from time to time; and in the progress of the needle, he caught glimpses of many aspects of this civilization, quite by chance: a food specialist preparing nutrient solutions; startling paintings in an art gallery; a machine scooping up dirt and transforming it to tunics, wire, and energy; a technician inseminating a chosen mother by the insertion of an analyzed and prepared sperm on a sterile injector; two children playing an intellectual game by rearranging the yellow, blue, and red cubes in a three-dimensional suspension; a clump of strange white trees, with branches drooping like the strands of an inverted mop, that lifted their roots and walked away from a region of drought toward a mountain lake.

The selector needle left the coast of Chile; and now the screen showed only the vacant waters of the Pacific. Graham remembered the latitude and longitude of Easter Island, and brought the selector to that area.

He saw Easter Island again, though its highest peak lay a hundred yards below the ocean surface. He saw it, for the vast column of alien energy had returned, driving the waters away. And in the crater of Rano Raraku, at the base of the implacable pillar, squatted the Keeper of the Seal, the green little statuette in a fury of mutation, pulsing and rioting through its cycle of expansions beyond the cosmos and contractions from other-time and other-space.

Graham looked at the screen with a dullness of despair. By the state of the pillar, he knew that at least another day would pass before the link was completely open for the titans to enter. He could, if he wished, fly to Easter Island and challenge the Keeper again.

He visualized himself engulfed once more by that abysmal force, to be hurled farther and farther onward in leaps of one and one-half million years, until he receded into conjectural vistas of vanishing time. For the measureless column, like the corridor at Stonehenge, was a time-trap, though of different kind; and unless the inventors of it, from their abode in the hyper-time and the hyper-space above and beyond the universe, chose to alter its function and the function of the Keeper, Graham could for ever take the action that would defer the completion of the link. And for ever and for ever he would be projected, in steps of one and one-half million years, intervals of absence and return, sliding down the utmost recesses of the future.

There was, of course, a method of escape at his disposal. He could walk to the Tower of Departure, and make his exit. He could abandon the world and all problems, all thinking.

But he would not, though he realized that all the long road he had travelled was yet to come. Perhaps, he thought, in one of his later absences, he would slip off the enigmatic ultracosmic beat within the vortex, slip off, not to return, but to emerge outside, in the workshop of the great chemists.

Graham opened the contact on the unitel set.

The screen went blank.

Three thousand copies of this book have been printed from linotype Baskerville by The Collegiate Press, George Banta Publishing Company, Menasha, Wisconsin. This book is printed on Winnebago Eggshell. The binding cloth is Holliston Black Novelex.